'**Samantha.**' Rafaele smiled. '**Aren't you going to ask me in? It's cold out here.**'

Sam's hand clenched tightly around the door. Panic rushed into her blood. Finally rousing her.

'Now isn't a good time. I thought I made it clear that I'm not interested.'

A dull flush accentuated Rafaele's cheekbones, but Sam was barely aware of it when she heard the high-pitched, *'Mummy!'* which was accompanied by small feet running at full speed behind her.

She felt Milo land at her legs and could almost visualise his little round face peeping out to see who was at the door. As if she were trying in vain to halt an oncoming train, Sam said in a thready voice, 'Now *really* isn't a good time.'

Rafaele stared at Milo for what seemed like an age. He frowned and then looked as if someone had just hit him in the belly. Dazed, he glanced up at Sam and she knew exactly what he was seeing. Her eyes were wide and stricken, set in a face leached of all colour.

Panicked. Gu

Just ice and

BLOOD BROTHERS

Power and passion run in their veins

Rafaele and Alexio have learned that to feel emotion is to be weak. Calculated ruthlessness brings them immense success in the boardroom and in the bedroom. But a storm is coming with the sudden appearance of a long-lost half-brother and three women who will change their lives for ever…

*Read **Rafaele Falcone's** story in:*
WHEN FALCONE'S WORLD STOPS TURNING
February 2014

Only one woman has come close to touching this brooding Italian's cold heart, and he intends to have her once more. But Samantha Rourke has a secret that will rock his world in a very different way…

*Read **Alexio Christakos's** story in:*
WHEN CHRISTAKOS MEETS HIS MATCH
April 2014

His legendary Greek charm can get him any woman he wants—and he wants Sidonie Fitzgerald for one, hot night. But when that night isn't enough will he regret breaking his own rules?

And coming soon…
***Cesar Da Silva's** story*
June 2014

The prodigal son is tormented by his dark past. Can one woman save this Spanish billionaire's tortured soul, or is he beyond redemption?

WHEN
FALCONE'S WORLD
STOPS TURNING

BY
ABBY GREEN

MILLS &
BOON

Published in Great Britain 2014
by Mills & Boon, an imprint of Harlequin (UK) Limited,
Eton House, 18-24 Paradise Road, Richmond, Surrey, TW9 1SR

© 2014 Abby Green

ISBN: 978 0 263 90825 1

Abby Green spent her teens reading Mills and Boon® romances. After repeatedly deferring a degree to study Social Anthropology (long story!) she ended up working for many years in the film and TV industry as an assistant director.

One day, while standing outside an actor's trailer waiting for him to emerge, in the rain, holding an umbrella in gale force winds, she thought to herself, *Surely there's more than this and it involves being inside and dry?*

Thinking of her love for Mills and Boon, and encouraged by a friend, Abby decided to submit a partial manuscript. After numerous rewrites, chucking out the original idea and starting again with a new story, her first book was accepted and an author was born.

She is happy to report that days of standing in the rain outside an actor's trailer are a rare occurrence now. She loves creating stories that will put the reader through an emotional wringer (in a good way, hopefully!), and yet leave her feeling satisfied and uplifted.

She lives in Dublin, Ireland, and you can find out more about her and her books here: www.abby-green.com

Recent titles by the same author:

FORGIVEN BUT NOT FORGOTTEN?
EXQUISITE REVENGE
ONE NIGHT WITH THE ENEMY
THE LEGEND OF DE MARCO

This is for Gervaise Landy, without whose influence I would most likely still be speaking into a walkie-talkie outside an actor's trailer in a car park somewhere, in the rain, trying to explain what the delay is. Thank you for all the great conversations about Mills & Boon, and that first memorable one in particular all those years ago. As soon as we recognised a fellow fanatic in each other we were kindred spirits. You were the one who put the idea in my head in the first place about writing for Mills & Boon, and you were the one with the tape on how to write one—which I still have, and which I will return to you as soon as you promise me you're going to sit down and finish that manuscript. With much love and thanks for sowing the seed of a dream in my head!

In thanking Gervaise I also have to dedicate this book to Caitríona Ní Mhurchú, at whose party I first met Gervaise. From the age of sixteen I have idolised this glamorous, confident, sexy, intelligent woman, so if you see any of those traits in my heroines it comes from a deep well of inspiration.

RAFAELE FALCONE LOOKED at the coffin deep inside the open grave. The earth they'd thrown in was scattered on top, along with some lone flowers left by departing friends and acquaintances. Some of them had been men, inordinately upset. Evidently there was some truth to the rumours that the stunning Esperanza Christakos had taken lovers during her third marriage.

Rafaele felt many conflicting emotions, apart from the obvious grief for his dead mother. He couldn't say that they'd ever had a close relationship; she'd been eternally elusive and had carried an air of melancholy about her. She'd also been beautiful. Beautiful enough to send his own father mad with grief when she left him.

The kind of woman who'd had the ability to make grown men completely lose all sense of dignity and of themselves. Not something that would ever happen to *him*. His single-minded focus was on his career and rebuilding the Falcone motor empire. Beautiful women were a pleasant diversion—nothing more. None of his lovers were ever under any illusions and expected nothing more than the transitory pleasure of his company.

His conscience pricked at this confident assertion—there had only been one lover who had taken him close to the edge but that was an experience he didn't dwell on… not any more.

His half-brother, Alexio Christakos, turned to him now and smiled tightly. Rafaele felt a familiar ache in his chest. He loved his half-brother, and had done from the moment he'd been born, but their relationship wasn't easy. It had been hard for Rafaele to witness his brother growing up, sure in the knowledge of his father's success and support—so different from his own experience with his father. He'd felt resentful for a long time, which hadn't been helped by his stepfather's obvious antipathy towards the son that wasn't his.

They both turned and walked away from the grave, engrossed in their own thoughts. Their mother had bequeathed to both her sons her distinctive green eyes, although Alexio's were a shade more golden than Rafaele's striking light green. Rafaele's hair was thicker and a darker brown next to his brother's short-cut ebony-black hair.

Differing only slightly in height, they were both a few inches over six foot. Rafaele's build was broad and powerful. His brother's just as powerful, but leaner. Dark stubble shadowed Rafaele's firm jawline today, and when they came to a stop near the cars Alexio observed it, remarking dryly, 'You couldn't even clean up for the funeral?'

The tightness in Rafaele's chest when he'd stood at the grave was easing slightly now. He curbed the urge to be defensive, to hide the vulnerability he felt, and faced his brother, drawling with a definite glint in his eye, 'I got out of bed too late.'

He couldn't explain to his brother how he'd instinctively sought the momentary escape he would find in the response of an eager woman, preferring not to dwell on how his mother's death had made him feel. Preferring not to dwell on how it had brought up vivid memories of when she'd walked out on his father so many years ago, leaving him a broken man. He was still bitter, adamantly refusing to pay his respects to his ex-wife today despite Rafaele's efforts to persuade him to come.

Alexio, oblivious to Rafaele's inner tumult, shook his head and smiled wryly. 'Unbelievable. You've only been in Athens for two days—no wonder you wanted to stay in a hotel and not at my apartment...'

Rafaele pushed aside the dark memories and quirked a mocking brow at his brother, about to dish out some of the same, when he saw a latecomer arrive. The words died on his lips and Alexio's smile faded as he turned to follow Rafaele's gaze.

A very tall, stern-faced stranger was staring at them both. And yet...he looked incredibly familiar. It was almost like looking into a mirror. Or at Alexio...if he had dark blond hair. It was his eyes, though, that sent a shiver through Rafaele. Green, much like his and Alexio's, except with a slight difference—a darker green, almost hazel. Another take on their mother's eyes...? But how could that be?

Rafaele bristled at this stranger's almost belligerent stance. 'May we help you?' he asked coolly.

The man's eyes flickered over them both, and then to the open grave in the distance. He asked, with a derisive curl to his lip, 'Are there any more of us?'

Rafaele looked at Alexio, who was frowning, and said, '*Us?* What are you talking about?'

The man looked at Rafaele. 'You don't remember, do you?'

The faintest of memories was coming back: he was standing on a doorstep with his mother. A huge imposing door was opening and there was a boy, a few years older than him, with blond hair and huge eyes.

The man's voice sounded rough in the still air. 'She brought you to my house. You must have been nearly three. I was almost seven. She wanted to take me with her then, but I wouldn't leave. Not after she'd abandoned me.'

Rafaele felt cold all over. In a slightly hoarse voice he asked, 'Who *are* you?'

The man smiled, but it didn't meet his eyes. 'I'm your older brother—*half-brother*. My name is Cesar Da Silva. I came today to pay my respects to the woman who gave me life...not that she deserved it. I was curious to see if any more would crawl out of the woodwork, but it looks like it's just us.'

Alexio erupted beside Rafaele. 'What the *hell*—?'

Rafaele was too stunned to move. He knew the Da Silva name. Cesar was behind the renowned and extremely successful Da Silva Global Corporation. His mind boggled to think that he might have met him and not known that they were brothers. With a sickening sense of inevitability, he didn't doubt a word this man had just said. Their fraternal similarities were too obvious. They could be non-identical triplets.

That half-memory, half-dream had always been all too real—he'd just never known for sure, because whenever he'd mentioned it to his mother she'd always changed the subject. Much in the way she had never discussed her life in her native Spain before she'd met his father in Paris, where she'd been a model.

Rafaele gestured to his brother, 'This is Alexio Christakos...our younger brother.'

Cesar Da Silva looked at him with nothing but ice in his eyes. 'Three brothers by three fathers...and yet she didn't abandon either of *you* to the wolves.'

He stepped forward then, and Alexio stepped forward too. The two men stood almost nose to nose, with Cesar topping his youngest brother in height only by an inch.

Cesar, his jaw as rigid as Alexio's, gritted out, 'I didn't come here to fight you, brother. I have no issue with either of you.'

Alexio's mouth thinned. 'Only with our dead mother, *if* what you say is true.'

Cesar smiled, but it was thin and bitter. 'Oh, it's true, all right — more's the pity.'

He stepped around Alexio then, and walked to the open grave. He took something out of his pocket and dropped it down into the dark space, where it fell onto the coffin with a distant hollow thud. He stood there for a long moment and then came back, his face expressionless.

After a charged silent moment between the three men he turned to stride away and got into the back of a waiting dark silver limousine, which moved off smoothly.

Rafaele turned to Alexio, who looked back at him, gob-smacked.

'What the...?' he trailed off.

Rafaele just shook his head. 'I don't know...'

He looked back to the space where the car had been and reeled with this cataclysmic knowledge.

CHAPTER ONE

Three months later...

'SAM, SORRY TO bother you, but there's a call for you on line one...someone with a very deep voice and a sexy foreign accent.'

Sam went very still. *Deep voice...sexy foreign accent.* The words sent a shiver of foreboding down her spine and a lick of something much hotter through her pelvis. She told herself she was being ridiculous and looked up from the results she'd been reading to see the secretary of the research department at the London university.

Kind eyes twinkled mischievously in a matronly face. 'Did you get up to something at the weekend? Or should I say some*one*?'

Again that shiver went down Sam's spine, but she just smiled at Gertie. 'Chance would be a fine thing. I spent all weekend working on Milo's playschool nature project with him.'

The secretary smiled and said indulgently, 'You know I live in hope, Sam. You and Milo need a gorgeous man to come and take care of you.'

Sam gritted her teeth and kept smiling, restraining herself from pointing out how well she and Milo were doing without a man. Now she couldn't wait to take the call. 'Did you say line one?'

Gertie winked and disappeared, and Sam took a deep breath before picking up the phone and pressing the flashing button. 'Dr Samantha Rourke here.'

There was silence for a few seconds, and then came the voice. Low, deep, sexy—and infinitely memorable. '*Ciao, Samantha, it's Rafaele...*'

The prickle of foreboding became a slap in the face. He was the only one apart from her father who had ever called her Samantha—unless it had been *Sam* in the throes of passion. All the blood in her body seemed to drain south, to the floor. Anger, guilt, emotional pain, lust and an awful treacherous tenderness flooded her in a confusing tumult.

She only realised she hadn't responded when the voice came again, cooler. 'Rafaele Falcone...perhaps you don't remember?'

As if that was humanly possible!

Her hand gripped the phone and she managed to get out, 'No... I mean, yes. I remember.'

Sam wanted to laugh hysterically. How could she forget the man when she looked into a miniature replica of his face and green eyes every day?

'*Bene,*' came the smooth answer. 'How are you, Sam? You're a doctor now?'

'Yes...' Sam's heart was doing funny things, beating so hard she felt breathless. 'I got my doctorate after...' She faltered and the words reverberated in her head unspoken. *After you came into my life and blew it to smithereens.* She fought valiantly for control and said in a stronger voice, 'I got my doctorate since I saw you last. How can I help you?'

Again a bubble of hysteria rose up in her: *how about helping him by telling him he has a son?*

'I am here in London because we've set up a UK base for Falcone Motors.'

'That's...nice,' Sam said, a little redundantly.

The magnitude of who she was talking to seemed to

hit her all of a sudden and she went icy all over. Rafaele Falcone. Here in London. He'd tracked her down. Why? *Milo.* Her son, her world. *His son.*

Sam's first irrational thought was that he must know, and then she forced herself to calm down. No way would Rafaele Falcone be calling her up sounding so blasé if he knew. She needed to get rid of him, though—fast. And then think.

'Look…it's nice to hear from you, but I'm quite busy at the moment…'

Rafaele's voice took on a cool edge again. 'You're not curious as to why I've contacted you?'

That sliver of fear snaked down Sam's spine again as an image of her adorable dark-haired son came into her mind's eye.

'I…well…I guess I am.' She couldn't have sounded less enthusiastic.

Rafaele's voice was almost arctic now. 'I was going to offer you a position with Falcone Motors. The research you're currently conducting is exactly in the area we want to develop.'

Sheer blind panic gripped Sam's innards at his words. She'd worked for this man once before and nothing had been the same since. Her tone frigid, she said, 'I'm afraid that's impossible. I'm committed to working on behalf of the university.'

Silence for a few taut seconds and then Rafaele responded with a terse, 'I see.'

Sam could tell that Rafaele had expected her to drop at his feet in a swoon of gratitude, even just at the offer of a job, if nothing more personal. It was the effect he had on most women. He hadn't changed. In spite of what had happened between them.

The words he'd left lingering in the air when he'd walked away from her resonated as if it had happened yesterday: *'It's for the best,* cara. *After all, it wasn't as if this was ever anything serious, was it?'*

He'd so obviously wanted her to agree with him that Sam had done so, in a flat and emotionless voice. Her body had seemed drained of all feeling. Relief had been a tangible force around him. It was something that she hadn't forgotten and which had helped her to believe she'd made the right decision to take full responsibility for Milo on her own. Even so, her conscience pricked her now: *you should have told him.*

Panic galvanised Sam, so that Rafaele Falcone's offer of a job barely impinged on her consciousness. 'Look, I really am quite busy. If you don't mind...?'

'You're not even interested in discussing this?'

Sam recalled the bile that had risen within her when Rafaele had made his uninterest in her all too clear and bit out curtly, 'No, I'm not interested. Goodbye, Signor Falcone.'

Goodbye, Signor Falcone, and this from a woman he knew intimately.

Rafaele looked at the phone in his hand for a long moment. Not comprehending the fact that she had just hung up on him. Women did not hang up on him.

Rafaele put the phone down and his mouth firmed. But Samantha Rourke had never been like other women. She'd been different from the start. He felt restless and got up from his seat to pace over to the huge window that overlooked operations at his new UK base on the outskirts of London. But for once his attention wasn't on operations.

She'd come to his factory in Italy as an intern after completing her Masters in Mechanical Automotive Engineering. The youngest and only woman in a group of men. Scarily bright and intelligent. He would have had no compunction hiring her on the spot and paying her whatever she asked just to keep her working for him…but he'd become distracted.

Distracted by her sexily studious air and her tall, slim body. Distracted by the mannish clothes she'd insisted on wearing which had made him want to peel them off to see the curves hinted at but hidden underneath. Distracted by her flawless pale Celtic skin and those huge almond-shaped eyes set in delicate features. Grey eyes…like a stormy sea.

Distracted by the way she would look at him and blush when he caught her eye, the way she would catch her lower lip between small white teeth. Distracted by that fall of inky black hair which she'd kept tucking behind her ear. And, as time had worn on, distracted by the slow-burning licking flames of desire that had grown hotter and stronger every time he saw her.

Rafaele had fought it. He hadn't liked it—and especially not in the workplace. There were plenty of females working in his factory and yet none of them had ever turned his head. His life was run on strict lines and he'd always kept his personal life well away from his work. But she had been so far removed from the kind of woman he normally went for: polished, sophisticated. Worldly wise. Women who were sexy and knew it and knew what to do with it. Cynical, like him.

Sam had been none of those things. Except sexy. And he'd known she didn't know that. She'd seemed to have absolutely no awareness of the fact that men's gazes lingered on her as she passed by. It had enraged Rafaele. The hot spurt of possessiveness had been an alien concept to him. Before they'd even kissed!

In the end sexual frustration had been such a tight ball of need inside him that one day he'd called her to his office and, without being able to say a word, had taken her

face in his hands and kissed her, drowning in an intoxicating sweetness he'd never tasted before.

Even now that memory alone had an effect on Rafaele's
libido and body. He cursed. He'd thought of her months
ago, at his mother's funeral. He thought of her more often
than he liked to admit. Sam was the one who had taken
him too close to the edge. They had shared more than just
a brief sexual history. They had almost shared...*a child*.

Even now a shiver of fear snaked down Rafaele's spine.
How close he'd come to dealing with something he never
wanted to deal with. That was what he needed to remember.

He swung around and stared blankly into his huge office. Clearly she wanted nothing to do with him, and he
should want to have nothing to do with her.

He should not have given in to the compulsion to track
her down. He should steer well clear of Samantha Rourke
and put her out of his mind. For good.

Samantha woke up on Saturday morning when a small
warm body burrowed into the bed beside her. She smiled
sleepily and wrapped her arms around her sturdy son,
breathing in his sweet scent.

'Morning, handsome.'

'Morning, Mummy, I love you.'

Sam's heart clenched so hard for a second that she
caught her breath. She kissed the top of his head. 'I love
you too, sweetheart.'

Milo pulled his head back and Sam cracked open an
eye and grimaced at the morning light.

He giggled. 'You're funny.'

Sam started to tickle Milo and he screeched with glee.
Soon they were both wide awake and he was scrambling
back out of the bed to clatter down the stairs.

She shouted after him. 'Don't turn on the TV yet!'

She heard him stop and could imagine his thwarted expression, and then he called back, 'Okay. I'll look at my book.'

Sam's heart clenched again. He would too. She knew when she went downstairs he'd be looking at his book studiously, even though he couldn't really read yet. He was such a good boy. Such a bright boy. Sometimes it scared her, how intelligent he was, because she felt as if she didn't have the means to handle it.

Bridie, her father's housekeeper, who had stayed on after he'd died two years previously, would often look at her with those far too shrewd Irish eyes and say, 'Well, where do you think he got it from? His grandfather was a professor of physics and you had your head in books from the age of two.'

Then she would sniff in that way she had and say, 'Now, obviously, as I don't know anything about his father, I can't speculate on that side of things...' which was Sam's cue to give her a baleful look and change the subject.

If it hadn't been for Bridie O'Sullivan, though, Sam reminded herself as she got out of bed, she would never have been able to get the PhD which had got her onto the lucrative research programme at the university, and which now helped pay for food, clothes *and* Bridie's wonderful care for Milo five days a week.

Bridie lived in the granny flat that had been built onto the side of the house some years before.

As Sam tied the belt on her robe, and prepared to go downstairs to get breakfast ready for herself and Milo, she tried to suppress the resurgence of guilt. The guilt that had been eating at her insides all week since she'd had *that* phone call. The guilt that had been a constant presence for four years, if she was completely honest with herself.

It unsettled her so much that she slept badly every night, tortured with memories while awake and by dreams while asleep, full of lurid images. *Hot* images. She woke tangled in the sheets, her skin damp with sweat, her heart racing, her head aching.

Rafaele Falcone. The man who had shown her just how colourless her world had been before demonstrating how easily he could deposit her back into perpetual greyness. As if she'd had no right to experience such a lavish, sensual dream.

Even now she wondered what on earth it had been about her that had caught his eye. But whatever it had been, to her everlasting shame, she would never forgive herself for believing that it had been more. For falling for him like some lovestruck teenager.

She reassured herself for the umpteenth time that week that he didn't deserve to know about Milo because he'd never wanted him in the first place. She would never forget how his face had leached of all colour when she'd told him she was pregnant.

Sam sagged back onto the side of the bed, the onslaught of memories coming too thick and fast to escape. He'd been away on a trip for three weeks and during that time Sam had found out she was pregnant. He'd asked to see her as soon as he'd returned, and after three weeks of no contact Sam hadn't been able to stop her heart from pumping with anticipation. Maybe he hadn't meant what he'd said before he'd gone on the trip…

'It might be no harm, cara, *for us to spend some time apart. My work is beginning to suffer…you're far too distracting…'*

But when she'd walked into his office he'd looked stern. Serious. Before she could lose her nerve Sam had blurted out, 'I have to tell you something.'

He'd looked at her warily. 'Go on, then.'

Sam had blushed and nervously twisted her hands, suddenly wondering if she was completely crazy to have a feeling of optimism that he might welcome her news. They'd only spent a month together. One heady, glorious month. Four weeks. Was that really enough time—?

'Sam?'

She'd looked at him, taken a deep breath and dived in. 'Rafaele…I'm pregnant.'

The words had hung ominously between them and a thick silence had grown. Rafaele's face had leached of all colour and Sam had known in that instant with cold clarity that she'd been a complete fool. About everything.

He'd literally gone white, his eyes standing out starkly green against the pallor. She'd thought he might faint and had moved towards him, but he'd put out a hand and asked hoarsely, 'How?'

She'd stopped in her tracks, but hadn't been able to halt the spread of ice in her veins. 'I think…when we were careless.'

An understatement for the amount of times they had been careless…in the shower, in the living room of Rafaele's *palazzo* when they'd been too impatient to make it to the bedroom, in the kitchen of her flat one evening, when he'd pushed her up against the counter and pulled down her trousers…

Sam had felt hot and mortified all at once. It felt so… *lurid* now. So desperate. It had been *sex*, not romance. Had she ever really known him? The vulnerability she'd felt in that moment was a searing everlasting memory.

He'd looked at her accusingly. 'You said you were on the pill.'

Sam got defensive. 'I was—I *am*. But I told you it was a low-dosage pill not specifically for contraception. And I had that twenty-four-hour bug a few weeks ago…'

Rafaele had sat down heavily into his chair. He looked as if he'd aged ten years in ten seconds. 'This can't be happening,' he'd muttered, as if Sam weren't even there.

She had tried to control her emotions, stop them from overwhelming her. 'It's as much of a shock to me as it obviously is to you.'

He'd looked up at her then and his face had tightened. 'Are you sure it's a shock? How do I know this wasn't planned in some attempt to trap me?'

Sam had almost staggered backwards, her mouth open, but nothing had come out. Eventually she'd managed, 'You think...you truly think I did this on purpose?'

Rafaele had stood up and started to pace, some colour coming back into his cheeks, highlighting that stunning bone structure. He'd laughed in a way that had chilled Sam right to her core, because she'd never heard him laugh like that before. Harsh.

He'd faced her. 'It's not unheard of, you know, for a woman who wants to ensure herself a lifetime of security from a rich man.'

The depth of this heretofore unrevealed cynicism had sent her reeling. Sam had stalked up to Rafaele's desk, her hands clenched to fists. 'You absolute *bastard*. I would never do such a thing.'

And then she'd had a flash of his expression and his demeanour when she'd come into the room, before she'd given him a chance to speak. A very bitter and dark truth had sunk in.

'You were going to tell me it was over, weren't you? That's why you asked to see me.'

Rafaele had had the grace to avoid her eye for a moment, but then he'd looked at her, his face devoid of expression.

'Yes.'

That was all. One word. Confirmation that Sam had been living in cloud cuckoo land, believing that what she'd shared with one of the world's perennial playboys had been *different*.

She'd been so overcome with conflicting emotions and turmoil at his attitude to her news and his stark lack of emotion that she'd been afraid if she tried to speak she'd start crying. So she'd run out of his office. Not even caring that she'd humiliated herself beyond all saving.

She'd hidden in her tiny apartment, avoiding Rafaele, avoiding his repeated attempts to get her to open the door.

And then it had started. The bleeding and the awful cramping pain. Terrified, Sam had finally opened the door to him, her physical pain momentarily eclipsing the emotional pain.

She'd looked at Rafaele and said starkly, 'I'm bleeding.'

He'd taken her to a clinic, grim and pale, but Sam hadn't really noticed. Her hands had been clutching her belly as she'd found herself willing the tiny clump of cells to live, no matter what. For someone who hadn't ever seriously contemplated having children, because she'd lost her own mother young and had grown up with an emotionally absent father, in that moment Sam had felt a primitive need to become a mother so strong that it had shaken her to her core.

At the clinic the kindly doctor had informed her that she wasn't, in fact, miscarrying. She was just experiencing heavier spotting than might be normal. He'd said the cramps were probably stress-induced and reassured her that with rest and avoiding vexatious situations she should go on to have a perfectly normal and healthy pregnancy.

The relief had been overwhelming. Until Sam had remembered that Rafaele was outside the door, pacing up and down, looking grim. He was a 'vexatious situation' personified. She could remember feeling the cramps come back even then, at the very prospect of having to deal with him, and again that visceral feeling had arisen: the need to protect her child.

She'd dreaded telling him that she hadn't miscarried after all.

And then a nurse had left the room, leaving the door ajar, and Rafaele's voice had floated distinctly into the room from just outside.

Everything within her stilling, Sam had heard him say tightly, *'I'm just caught up with something at the moment... No, it's not important... I will resolve this as soon as I can and get back to you.'*

And just like that the small, traitorous flame of hope she'd not even been aware she was pathetically harbouring had been extinguished. Obviously because of doctor/patient confidentiality Rafaele was none the wiser as to whether or not she'd actually miscarried. He believed that she had.

He'd terminated his conversation and come into the room. Sam had looked out of the window, feeling as if she was breaking apart inside. She'd forced herself to be calm and not stressed. The baby was paramount now.

Rafaele had stopped by the bed. 'Sam...'

Sam hadn't looked at him. She'd just answered, 'What?'

She'd heard him sigh. 'Look, I'm sorry...really sorry that this has happened. We should never have become involved.'

Sam had felt empty. 'No,' she'd agreed, 'we shouldn't have.'

Even then a small voice had urged her to put him straight, but she'd felt so angry in that moment and had already felt her stress levels rising, her body starting to cramp. Dangerous for the baby.

Feeling panicked, she'd finally turned her head to acknowledge Rafaele and said, 'Look, what's done is done. It's over. I have to stay in for a night for observation but I'm leaving tomorrow. I'm going home.'

Rafaele had been pale but Sam had felt like reaching

up to slap him. He felt no more for her than he did for the fact that as far as he was aware he'd just lost a baby. He just wanted to be rid of her. *'I will resolve this as soon as I can...'*

'Just go, Rafaele, leave me be.' *Please,* she'd begged silently, feeling those stress levels rising. Her hands had tightened on the bedcover, knuckles white.

Rafaele had just looked at her, those green eyes unfathomable. 'It's for the best, *cara.* Believe me... You are young...you have your career ahead of you. After all, it wasn't as if this was ever anything serious, was it?'

Sam's mouth had twisted and she'd resolved in that moment to do her utmost to focus on her career...and her baby. No matter what it took. 'Of course not. Now, please, just *go.*'

Sam's control had felt so brittle she'd been afraid it would snap at any moment and he'd see the true depth of her agony.

Rafaele had stepped back a pace. 'I will arrange for your travel home. You won't have to worry about anything.'

Sam had stifled a semi-hysterical giggle at the thought of the monumental task and life-change ahead of her. She'd nodded abruptly. 'Fine.'

Rafaele had been almost at the door by then, relief a tangible aura around him. 'Goodbye, Sam.'

Feeling a sob rise, and choking it down with all of her will and strength, Sam had managed a cool-sounding, 'Goodbye, Rafaele.' And then she'd turned her head, because her eyes had been stinging. She'd heard the door close softly and a huge sob had ripped out of her chest, and tears, hot and salty, had flowed down her cheeks.

By the time Sam had been at home for a week she'd begun veering wildly between the urge to tell Rafaele the truth and the urge to protect herself from further pain. Then she'd seen on some vacuous celebrity TV channel that Rafaele was already out and about with some gorgeous Italian TV personality, smiling that devilishly sexy smile. As she'd looked at Rafaele, smiling for the TV cameras, his arm around the waist of the sinuous dark-haired Latin beauty, she'd known that she could never tell him because he simply wasn't interested.

'*Mummy, I want Cheerios!*'

Sam blinked and came back to reality. Milo. Breakfast. She pushed aside the memories, tried to ignore the guilt and got up to attend to her son.

That evening when the doorbell rang Sam looked up from washing the dinner things in the sink. Milo was playing happily on the floor in the sitting room with his cars, oblivious. As she went to answer it she assured herself it was probably just Bridie, who had forgotten her keys to the flat again.

But when she opened the door on the dusky late winter evening it wasn't Bridie, who stood at five foot two inches in heels. It was someone over a foot taller and infinitely more masculine.

Rafaele Falcone.

For a long, breathless moment, the information simply wouldn't compute. Suspended in time, Sam seemed to be able to take in details almost dispassionately. Faded jeans. Battered leather jacket. Thin wool jumper. Thick dark brown hair which still had a tendency to curl a little too much over his collar. The high forehead. The deep-set startling green eyes. The patrician bump of his nose, giving him that indelible air of arrogance. The stunning bone structure and that golden olive skin that placed him somewhere more exotic than cold, wet England.

And his mouth. That gorgeous, sculpted-for-wicked-things mouth. It always looked on the verge of tipping into a sexy half-smile, full of the promise of sensual nirvana.

Unless it was pulled into a grim line, as it had been when she had seen him last.

Reality slammed into Sam like a fist to her gut. She actually sucked in a breath, only realising then that she'd been starving her lungs for long seconds while she gawped at him like a groupie.

'Samantha.'

His voice lodged her even more firmly in reality. And the burning intensity of his green eyes as they swept down her body. Sam became acutely aware of her weekend uniform of skinny jeans, thick socks and a very worn plaid shirt. Her hair was scraped up into a bun and she wore no make-up.

Rafaele smiled. 'Still a tomboy, I see. Despite my best efforts.'

A memory exploded into Sam's consciousness. Rafaele, in his *palazzo*, presenting her with a huge white box. Under what had seemed like acres and acres of silver tissue paper a swathe of material had appeared.

Sam had lifted it out to reveal a breathtaking evening gown. Rafaele had stripped her himself and dressed her again. One-shouldered and figure-hugging, in black and flesh-coloured stripes, the dress had accentuated her hips, her breasts, and a long slit had revealed her legs. Then he'd taken her out to one of Milan's most exclusive restaurants. They'd been the last to leave, somewhere around four o'clock in the morning, drunk on sparkling wine and lust, and he'd taken her home to his *palazzo*…

'Still a tomboy, I see…'

The memory vanished and the backdrop of Sam's very suburban street behind Rafaele came back into view.

Sexy smile. 'Aren't you going to ask me in? It's cold out here.'

Sam's hand clenched tight around the door. *Milo*. Panic rushed into her blood. Finally. Rousing her.

'Now isn't a good time. I don't know why you've come here. I thought I made it clear the other day that I'm not interested.'

Sam forced herself to look at him. Four years had passed and in that time she'd changed utterly. She felt older, more jaded. Whereas Rafaele only looked even more gorgeous. The unfairness of it galvanised her. He'd known nothing of her life the last few years. *Because you didn't tell him*, a voice pointed out.

'Why did you come here, Rafaele? I'm sure you have more important things to do on a Saturday evening.'

The bitterness in Sam's voice surprised her.

Rafaele's jaw tightened, but he answered smoothly. 'I thought if I came to see you in person you might be persuaded to listen to my offer.'

A dull flush accentuated Rafaele's cheekbones, but Sam was barely aware of it as she heard a high-pitched 'Mummy!' which was accompanied by small feet running at full speed behind her.

She felt Milo land at her legs, clasping his arms around them, and could almost visualise his little round face peeping out to see who was at the door. Like trying in vain to halt an oncoming train, Sam said in a thready voice, 'Like I said, now really isn't a good time.'

She could see awareness dawn on Rafaele's face as he obviously took in the fact of a child. He started to speak stiltedly. 'I'm sorry. I should have thought... Of course it's been years...you must be married by now. Children...'

Then his eyes slid down and she saw them widen. She didn't have to look to know that Milo was now standing beside her, one chubby hand clinging onto her leg. Wide green eyes would be staring innocently up into eyes the exact same shade of green. Unusual. Lots of people commented on how unusual they were.

Rafaele stared at Milo for what seemed like an age. He

frowned and then looked as if someone had just hit him in the belly...dazed. He looked up at Sam and she knew exactly what he was seeing as clearly as if she was standing apart, observing the interplay. Her eyes were wide and stricken, set in a face leached of all colour. Pale as parchment. Panicked. *Guilty.*

And just like that, something in his eyes turned to ice and she knew that he knew.

CHAPTER TWO

'MUMMY, CAN WE watch the cars on TV now?'

Sam put her hand to Milo's head and said faintly, 'Why don't you go on and I'll be there in a minute, okay?'

Milo ran off again and the silence grew taut between Sam and Rafaele. He knew. She felt it in her bones. He'd known as soon as he'd looked into his son's eyes. So identical. She hated that something about his immediate recognition of his own son made something soften inside her.

He was looking at her so hard she felt it like a physical brand on her skin. Hot.

'Let me in, Samantha. Now.'

Feeling shaky and clammy all at once, Sam stepped back and opened the door. Rafaele came in, his tall, powerful form dwarfing the hallway. He smelt of light spices and something musky, and through the shock Sam's blood jumped in recognition.

She shut the door and walked quickly to the kitchen at the end of the hall, passing where Milo sat cross-legged in front of the TV watching a popular car programme. His favourite.

She was about to pull the door shut when a curt voice behind her instructed, 'Leave it.'

She dropped her hand and tensed. Rafaele was looking at Milo as he sat enraptured by the cars on the screen. He was holding about three of his favourite toy cars in his hands. If his eyes and pale olive skin hadn't been a fatal giveaway then this might have been the worst kind of ironic joke.

Sam stepped back and walked into the kitchen. She couldn't feel her legs. She felt sick, light-headed. She turned around to see Rafaele follow her in and close the door behind him, not shutting it completely.

Rafaele was white beneath his dark colouring. And he looked murderous.

He bit out, 'This is where you tell me that by some extraordinary feat of genetic coincidence that little boy in there *isn't* three years and approximately three months old. That he *didn't* inherit exactly the same colour eyes that I inherited from my own mother. That he *isn't* my son.'

Sam opened her mouth. 'He is...' Even now, at this last second, her brain searched desperately for something to cling onto. Some way this could be justified. *He was his father.* She couldn't do it. She didn't have the right any more. She'd never had the right. 'He is your son.'

Silence, stretching taut and stark, and then he repeated, 'He is my son?'

Sam just nodded. Nausea was churning in her belly now. The full implications of this were starting to hit home.

Rafaele emitted a long stream of Italian invective and Sam winced because she recognised some of the cruder words—they were pretty universal. Her belly was so tight she put a hand to it unconsciously. She watched as Rafaele struggled to take this in. The enormity of it.

'No wonder you were so keen to get rid of me the other day.'

He paced back and forth in the tiny space. She could feel his anger and tension as it lashed out like a live electrical wire, snapping at her feet.

Suddenly he stopped and looked at her. 'Are you married?'

Sam shook her head painfully. 'No.'

'And what if I hadn't decided to pay you a visit? Would you have let me remain in blissful ignorance for ever?'

Stricken, Sam whispered, 'I don't…I don't know.' Even as she admitted that, though, the knowledge seeped in. She wouldn't have been able to live with the guilt. She would have told him.

He pinned her to the spot with that light green gaze which had once devoured her alive and was now colder than the arctic.

'You bitch.'

Sam flinched. He might as well have slapped her across the face. It had the same effect. The words were so coldly and implacably delivered.

'You didn't want a baby,' she whispered, unable to inject more force into her voice.

'So you just lied to me?'

Sam could feel her cheeks burning now, with shame. 'I thought it was a miscarriage, as did you. But at the clinic, after the doctor had done his examination, he told me that I wasn't miscarrying.'

Rafaele crossed his arms and she could see his hands clenched to fists. She shivered at the threat of violence even though she knew he would never hit her. But she sensed he wanted to hit something.

'You knew then and yet you barefaced lied to me and let me walk away.'

Clutching at the smallest of straws, Sam said shakily, 'I didn't lie…you assumed…I just didn't tell you.'

'And the reason you didn't inform me was because…?'

'You didn't…didn't want to know.' The words felt flimsy and ineffectual now. Petty.

'Based on…?'

It was as if he couldn't quite get out full sentences, Sam felt his rage strangling his words.

Her brain felt heavy. 'Because of how you reacted when I told you in the first place...'

Sam recalled the indescribable pain of realising that Rafaele had been about to break it off with her. His abject shock at the prospect of her pregnancy. It gave her some much needed strength. 'And because of what you said afterwards...at the clinic. I heard you on the phone.'

Rafaele frowned and it was a glower. 'What did I say?'

Sam's sliver of strength started to drain away again like a traitor. 'You were talking to someone. You said you were caught up in something *unimportant*.' Even now those words scored at Sam's insides like a knife.

Rafaele's expression turned nuclear. His arms dropped, his hands were fists. '*Dio*, Samantha. I can't even recall that conversation. No doubt I just said something—anything—to placate one of my assistants. I thought you'd just miscarried. Do you really think I was about to announce *that* in an innocuous phone call?'

Sam gulped and had to admit reluctantly, 'Maybe... maybe not. But how did I know that? All I could hear was your relief that you didn't have to worry about a baby holding your life up and your eagerness to leave.'

He all but exploded. 'Need I remind you that I was also in shock, and at that point I thought there was no baby!'

Sam was breathing hard and Rafaele looked as if he was about to kick aside the kitchen table between them to come and throttle her.

Just then a small, unsure voice emerged from the doorway. 'Mummy?'

Immediately Sam's world refracted down to Milo, who stood in the doorway. He'd opened it unnoticed by them and was looking from one to the other, his lower lip quivering ominously at the explosive tension.

Sam flew over and picked him up and he clung to her.

Her conscience struck her. He was always a little intimidated by men because he wasn't around them much.

'Why is the man still here?' he asked now, slanting sidelong looks to Rafaele and curling into Sam's body as much as he could.

Sam stroked his back reassuringly and tried to sound normal. 'This is just an old friend of Mummy's. He's stopped by to say hello, that's all. He's leaving now.'

'Okay,' Milo replied, happier now. 'Can we look at cars?'

Sam looked at him and forced a smile, 'Just as soon as I say goodbye to Mr Falcone, okay?'

'Okey-dokey.' Milo used his new favourite phrase that he'd picked up in playschool, squirmed back out of Sam's arms and ran out of the kitchen again.

Sam watched Rafaele struggle to take it all in. Myriad explosive emotions crossing his face.

'You'll have to go,' she entreated. 'It'll only confuse and upset him if you stay.'

Rafaele closed the distance between them and Sam instinctively moved back, but the oven was behind her. Rafaele's scent enveloped her, musky and male. Her heart pounded.

'This is not over, Samantha. I'll leave now, because I don't want to upset the boy, but you'll be hearing from me.'

After a long searing moment, during which she wasn't sure how she didn't combust from the anger being directed at her, Rafaele turned on his heel and left, stopping briefly at the sitting room door to look in at Milo again.

He cast one blistering look back at Sam and then he was out through the front door and gone. Sam heard the powerful throttle of an engine as it roared to life and then mercifully faded again.

It was then that she started to shake all over. Grasping

for a chair to hold onto, she sank down into it, her teeth starting to chatter.

'Mummeeee!' came a plaintive wail from the sitting room.

Sam called out, 'I'll be there in one second, I promise.'

The last thing she needed was for Milo to see her in this state. Her brain was numb. She couldn't even quite take in what had just happened—the fact that she'd seen Rafaele again for the first time since those cataclysmic days.

When she was finally feeling a little more in control she went in to Milo and sat down on the floor beside him. Without even taking his eyes off the TV he crawled into her lap and Sam's heart constricted. She kissed his head.

Rafaele's words came back to her: *This is not over, Samantha. I'll leave now, because I don't want to upset the boy, but you'll be hearing from me.*

She shivered. She didn't even want to think of what she'd be facing when she heard from Rafaele again.

On Monday morning Sam filed into the conference room at the university and took a seat at the long table for the weekly budget meeting. Her eyes were gritty with tiredness. Unsurprisingly she hadn't slept all weekend, on tenterhooks waiting for Rafaele to appear again like a spectre. In her more fanciful moments she'd imagined that she'd dreamt it all up: the phone call; his appearance at the house. *Coming face to face with his son.* A small, snide voice pointed out that it was no less than she deserved but she pushed it down.

Robustly she told herself that if she'd had to go back in time she would have done the same again, because if she hadn't surely the stress of Rafaele being reluctantly bound to her and a baby would have resulted in a miscarriage for real?

Gertie, the secretary, arrived then and sat down breathlessly next to Sam. She said urgently, 'You'll never guess what's happened over the weekend…'

Sam looked at her, used to Gertie's penchant for gossip. She didn't want to hear some salacious story involving students and professors behaving badly, but the older woman's face suddenly composed itself and Sam looked to see that the head of their department had walked into the room.

And then her heart stopped. Because right on his heels was another man. *Rafaele.*

For a second Sam thought she might faint. She was instantly light-headed. She had to put her hands on the edge of the table and grip it as she watched in mounting horror and shock as Rafaele coolly and calmly strode into the room, looking as out of place in this unadorned academic environment as an exotic peacock on a grubby high street.

He didn't even glance her way. He took a seat at the head of the table alongside their boss, looking stupendously handsome and sexy. He sat back, casually undoing a button on his pristine suit jacket with a big hand, long fingers…

Sam was mesmerised.

This had to be a dream, she thought to herself frantically. She'd wake up any moment. But Gertie was elbowing her none too discreetly and saying *sotto voce*, 'This is what I was about to tell you.'

The stern glare of their boss quelled any chat and then, with devastating inevitability, Sam's stricken gaze met Rafaele's and she knew it wasn't a dream. There was a distinct gleam of triumph in those green depths, and a more than smug smile was playing around that firmly sculpted mouth.

Her boss was standing up and clearing his throat. Sam couldn't look away from Rafaele, and he didn't remove his gaze from hers, as if forcing her to take in every word now being spoken, but she only heard snippets.

'Falcone Industries…most successful…honoured that

Mr Falcone has decided to fund this research out of his own pocket...delighted at this announcement...funding guaranteed for as long as it takes.'

Then Rafaele got up to address the room. There were about thirteen people and, predictably, you could have heard a pin drop as his charismatic effect held everyone in thrall. He'd finally moved his gaze from Sam and she felt as if she could breathe again, albeit painfully. Her heart was racing and she took in nothing of what he said, trying to wrap her sluggish brain around the ramifications of this shocking development.

'*Samantha...'*

Sam looked up, dazed, to see her boss was now addressing her, and that Rafaele had sat down. She hadn't noticed, nor heard a word.

'I'm sorry, Bill, what did you say?' She was amazed she'd managed to speak.

'I *said*,' he repeated with exaggerated patience, clearly disgruntled that she appeared to be on another planet while in such illustrious company, 'that as of next week you will be working from the Falcone factory. You're to oversee setting up a research facility there which will work in tandem with the one here in the university.'

He directed himself to the others again while this bomb detonated within Sam's solar plexus.

'I don't think I need to point out the significance of being allowed to conduct this research within a functioning factory, and especially one as prestigious as Falcone Motors. It'll put us streets ahead of other research in this area and, being assured of Falcone funding for at least five years, we're practically guaranteed success.'

Sam couldn't take any more. She rose up in a blind panic, managed to mumble something vague about needing air and fled the room.

* * *

Rafaele watched Sam leave dispassionately. Since the other evening he'd been in shock. Functioning, but in shock. His anger and rage was too volcanic to release, fearsome in its intensity. And fearsome for Rafaele if he contemplated for a second why his emotions were so deep and hot.

Sam's boss beside him emitted a grunt of displeasure at her hasty departure, but Rafaele felt nothing but satisfaction to be causing her a modicum of the turbulence in his own gut. Through his shock Rafaele had felt a visceral need to push Sam off her axis as much as she'd pushed him off his.

He recalled bitterly how reluctant she'd been to talk to him in the first place about the job he was offering, all the while knowing her secret. Harbouring his son. With one phone call to his team Rafaele had put in motion this audacious plan to take over the research programme at her university and had relished this meeting.

While Sam's boss continued his speech Rafaele retreated inwardly, but anyone looking at him would have seen only fierce concentration.

He breathed in and realised that he hadn't taken a proper breath since he'd seen Sam looking at him with that stricken expression on her face in the doorway of her house the other evening. The initial punch to his gut he'd received when he'd first thought that Sam was married, with someone else's child, was galling to remember—and more exposing than he liked to admit.

Nothing excused her from withholding his son from him for more than three years. Rafaele had been about Milo's age when his world had imploded. When he'd witnessed his father, on his knees, sobbing, prostrating himself at Rafaele's mother's feet, begging her not to leave him.

'I love you. What am I if you leave? I am nothing. I have nothing...'

'Get up, Umberto,' she'd said. *'You shame yourself in front of our son. What kind of a man will he be with a crying, snivelling wretch for a father?'*

What kind of a man would he be?

Rafaele felt tight inside. The kind of man who knew that the most important things in life were building a solid foundation. Security. Success. He'd vowed never to allow anything to reduce him to nothing, as his father had been reduced, with not even his pride to keep him standing. Emotions were dangerous. They had the power to derail you completely. He knew how fickle women were, how easily they could walk away. Or keep you from your child.

Rafaele had driven back to Sam's house on Sunday, fired up, ready to confront her again, but just as he'd pulled up he'd seen them leaving the house. Milo had been pushing a scooter. He'd followed them to a small local park and watched like a fugitive as they played. Dark emotions had twisted inside him as he'd watched Sam's effortless long-legged grace and ease. He'd known that if he hadn't reappeared in their lives this would have just been another banal Sunday morning routine trip to the park.

Seeing his son's small sturdy body, watching him running around, laughing gleefully, something alien inside him had swelled. It was…pride. And something else that he couldn't name. But it had reminded him of that day again—the darkest in his memory—when his mother had gripped his hand painfully tight and pulled him in her wake out of their family *palazzo* outside Milan, leaving his father sobbing uncontrollably on the ground. A pathetic, broken man.

That was one of the reasons Rafaele had never wanted to have children. Knowing how vulnerable they were had always felt like too huge a responsibility to bear. No one knew better than he how events even at that young age could shape your life. And so he'd never expected that, when faced with his son, there would be such a torrent of feelings within him, each one binding him invisibly and indelibly to this person he didn't even know properly yet. Or that when he'd watched him running around the other day there would be a surge of something so primal and protective that he just knew without question, instantly, that he would do anything to prevent his son from coming into harm's way.

From far too early an age Rafaele had been made aware that the absence of a father corroded at your insides like an acid.

Resolve firmed like a ball of concrete inside him. There was no way on this earth that he was going to walk away from his son now and give him a taste of what he'd suffered.

Cutting off Sam's boss curtly, Rafaele stood up and muttered an excuse, and left the room. There was only one person he wanted to hear talk right now.

Sam's stomach felt raw after she'd lost her breakfast, minute as it had been, into a toilet in the ladies' room. She felt shaky, weak, and looked as pale as death in the reflection of the cracked mirror. She splashed water on her face and rinsed her mouth out, knowing that she had to go back out there and face—

The door suddenly swung open and Sam stood up straight, hands gripping the side of the sink. For once she prayed it might be Gertie, even though she knew it wasn't when every tiny hair seemed to prickle on her skin.

She turned around and saw Rafaele, looking very tall and very dark as he leant back against the door, hands thrust deep into his pockets. Even now her body sang, recognising the man who had introduced her to her own sensuality, and she clamped down on the rogue response, bitterly aware that not even the harsh fluorescent lighting could strip away his sheer good looks.

Welcome anger rose up and Sam seized on it, crossing her arms over her chest. Her voice felt rough, raw. 'What the hell do you think you're playing at, Rafaele? How dare you come in here and use your might to get back at me? These are people you're playing with—people who have invested long years of study into their area—and suddenly you sweep in and promise them a glimpse of future success when we both know—'

'Enough.'

Rafaele's voice sounded harsh in the echoing silence of the cavernous tiled ladies' bathroom.

'I am fully committed to following through on my promise of funding and support to this university.' His mouth tightened. 'Unless you've already forgotten, I *had* contacted you initially to ask you to work for me. I had every intention of using your expertise to further this very research for my own ends.'

He shrugged minutely. 'There's nothing new in that—any motor company worth its salt is on the lookout for new research and ways of beating the competition with new technology. You have single-handedly elevated this research to a far more advanced level than any other facility, in a university or otherwise.'

His words sent Sam no sense of professional satisfaction. She was still in shock. 'That may be the case,' she bit out tightly, 'but now that you know about Milo you're seeking to get back at me personally.'

She couldn't keep the bitterness from her voice.

'It just so happens that you have the means to be able to come in and take over the entire department to do your bidding.'

Fresh panic gripped her when she recalled her boss saying something about Sam herself going to work from his factory. Her arms grew tighter over her chest when she recalled the hothouse environment of working in Rafaele's Milan factory four years ago and how easily he'd seduced her. The thought of going back into a similar environment, even if Rafaele would prefer to throttle her than sleep with her, made her clammy.

'I will not be going to work for you. I will remain here at the university.'

Rafaele took a few paces forward and Sam saw the light of something like steel in his eyes and his expression. Her belly sank even as her skin tightened with betraying awareness.

'You *will* be coming to work for me—or I will pull out of this agreement and all of your colleagues are back to square one. Your boss has informed me that if I hadn't come along with the promise of funding he was going to have to let some people go. He can't keep everyone on the payroll due to reduced projected funding this year. You would have been informed of that at this very meeting.'

Vaguely Sam was aware of the veracity of what he said. It had been rumoured for weeks. Once again she was struck by how little she'd appreciated how ruthless Rafaele was. 'You bastard,' she breathed.

Rafaele looked supremely unperturbed. 'Hardly, when I'm saving jobs. It's very simple if you do the right thing and accede to my wishes. And this is just the start of it, Samantha.'

Ice invaded her bloodstream. 'Start of what?'

To her shock she realised belatedly how close Rafaele had come when he reached out a hand and cupped her jaw. She felt the strength of that hand, the faint calluses which reminded her of how he loved tinkering with engines despite his status. It was one of the things that had endeared him to her from the start.

In an instant an awful physical yearning rose up within

her. Every cell in her body was reacting joyously to a touch she'd never thought she'd experience again. She was melting, getting hot. Damp.

Softly, he sliced open the wound in her heart. 'The start of payback, Samantha. You owe me for depriving me of my son for more than three years and I will never let you forget it.'

For a moment Rafaele almost forgot where he was, who he was talking to. The feel of Sam's skin under his hand was like silk, her jaw as delicate as the finest spun Murano glass. He had an almost overwhelming urge to keep sliding his hand around to the back of her neck, to tug her towards him so that he could feel her pressed against him and crush that pink rosebud mouth under his— Suddenly Rafaele realised what he was doing.

With a guttural curse he took his hand away and stepped back. Sam was looking at him with huge grey eyes, her face as pale as parchment with two pink spots in each cheek.

She blinked, almost as if she'd been caught in a similar spell, and then something in her eyes cleared. The anger was gone.

She changed tack, entreated him. She held out a hand and her voice was husky. 'Please, Rafaele, we need to talk about this—'

'No.' The word was harsh, abrupt, and it cut her off effectively. Everything within Rafaele had seized at her attempt to try and take advantage of a moment when she might have perceived weakness on his part. To play on his conscience. With the shadows under her eyes making her look fragile and vulnerable.

He'd witnessed his mother for years, using her wiles to fool men into thinking she was vulnerable, fragile. Only to see how her expression would harden again once they were no longer looking and she'd got what she wanted. She'd been so cold the day she'd left his father, showing not an ounce of remorse.

Once, he mightn't have believed Sam was like that, but that was before she'd kept his son from him, demonstrating equal, if not worse, callousness.

Rafaele took another step back and hated that he felt the need to do so. That volcanic anger was well and truly erupting now. He gritted out, 'If you were a man...'

Sam tensed and her chin lifted. Gone was the soft look of before, the husky entreaty.

'If I were a man...what? You'd thrash me? Well, what's stopping you?'

Rafaele could see where her hands had clenched to fists by her side. He looked at her disgustedly. 'Because I don't raise my hands to women—or anyone, for that matter. But I felt like it for the first time when I realised that boy was my son.'

He couldn't stop the words spilling out. That initial shock was infusing him all over again.

'My *son*, Sam, my flesh and blood. He's a Falcone. *Dio*. How could you have played God like that? What gave you the right to believe you had the answer? That you alone could decide to just cut me out of his life?'

Sam seemed to tense even more, her chin going higher. Those spots of red deepened, highlighting her delicate bone structure. 'Do I need to remind you *again* that you practically tripped over your feet in your hurry to get out of the clinic that day? You could barely disguise your relief when you thought there was nothing to worry about. You just assumed the worst. It didn't even occur to you to question whether or not I'd actually had a miscarriage, because you didn't want a baby.'

Rafaele coloured, his conscience pricked by the reminder of how eager he'd been to get away from those

huge bruised eyes, the raw emotion. The shock. The awareness that Sam had strayed too far under his skin.

Tightly he admitted, 'I never had any intention of having children. But you gave me no reason to doubt the inevitable conclusion of what we'd both believed to be a
miscarriage.'

Sam choked out, 'You were quite happy to wash your
hands of me, so don't blame me now if I felt the best course
was to leave you out of my decision-making process.'

Rafaele looked at Sam across the few feet that separated
them and all he could see was her eyes. Huge, and as grey
as the rolling English clouds. She was sucking him in again
but he wouldn't let her. She'd wilfully misdirected him into
believing she'd miscarried when all the while she'd held
the knowledge of their baby, *living*, in her belly.

He shook his head. 'That's just not good enough.'

Sam's voice took on a defensive edge. 'I was hardly
encouraged to get in touch and tell you the truth when I
saw you with another woman only a week after that day.'

She was breathing heavily under her shirt and he could
see her breasts rise and fall. A flash of heat went straight
to his groin and Rafaele crushed it ruthlessly. He focused
on her face and tried to forget that he actually hadn't slept
with another woman for about a year after Sam had left,
despite appearances and despite his best efforts. Every
time he'd come close something inside him had shut down.
And since then…? His experiences with women had been
anything but satisfactory. To be reminded of this now was
galling.

He narrowed his eyes. 'Don't you dare try to put this
on me now, just to deflect your own guilt.'

But the guilt that had struck Rafaele wouldn't be ban-
ished, much as he wanted it to be. Damn her! He wouldn't
let her do this to him now. She'd borne his child. His son.
And said nothing.

Sam's voice was bitter. 'God forbid that I would forget what our relationship was about. *Sex.* That was pretty much it, wasn't it? Forget conversation, or anything more intimate than being naked in bed. It wasn't as if you didn't make that abundantly clear, Rafaele, telling me over and over again not to fall for you because you weren't *about* that.'

'But you did anyway, didn't you?' Rafaele couldn't keep the accusing note out of his voice and he saw Sam blanch.

'I thought I loved you.' Her mouth twisted. 'After all, you were my first lover, and isn't it normal for a virgin to develop an attachment to her first? Isn't that one of the helpful warnings you gave me?'

Rafaele saw nothing right then but a memory of Sam's naked and flushed body as she'd lain on his bed before him, her breasts high and round, her narrow waist, long legs. Skin so pure and white it had reminded him of alabaster—except she'd been living, breathing, so passionate. And she'd been innocent. He'd never forget how it had felt to sink into that slick, tight heat for the first time. It was his most erotic memory. Her gasp of shock turning to pleasure.

She continued, 'But don't worry. I soon got over it and realised how shallow those feelings were. Once I was faced with the reality of pregnancy and a baby.'

'A reality,' Rafaele gritted out, angry at that memory and at how easily it had slipped past his guard, 'that you decided to face *alone.*'

Reacting against her ability to scramble his thought-processes, Rafaele changed tack.

'Was it a punishment, Sam? Hmm?' He answered himself. 'Punishment for my being finished with you? For not wanting more? For letting you go? For not wanting to have a baby because that's not what our relationship was about?'

Rafaele couldn't stop the demon inside him.

'I think the problem is that you fell for me and you were angry because I didn't fall for you, so you decided to punish me. It's so obvious…'

[illegible faded text from previous page showing through]

CHAPTER THREE

SAM CLOSED the distance between them, her hand lifted and she hit Rafaele across the face before she even registered the impulse to do so. She realised in the sickeningly taut silence afterwards that she'd reacted because he'd spoken her worst fears out loud. Here in this awful, stark, echoey room.

With a guttural curse, and his cheek flaring red where Sam had hit him, Rafaele hauled her into his arms and his mouth was on hers. He was kissing her angrily, roughly.

It took a second for Sam to get over the shock, but what happened next wasn't the reaction she would have chosen if she'd had half a brain cell still working. Her reaction came from her treacherous body and overrode her brain completely.

She started kissing him back, matching his anger with her own. For exposing her. For saying those words out loud. For making her feel even more ashamed and confused. For being *here*. For making her want him. For making her remember. For kissing her just to dominate her and prove how much she still wanted him.

Her hands were clutching Rafaele's jacket. She tasted blood and yet it wasn't pain that registered. It was passion, and it sent her senses spiralling out of all control. Rafaele's hands were bruisingly hard on her arms and tears pricked behind Sam's eyelids at the tumult of desire mixed with frustration.

She opened her eyes to see swirling green oceans. Rafaele pulled away jerkily and Sam could hear nothing but the thunder of her own heartbeat and her ragged breathing. She was still clutching his jacket and she let go, her hands shaking.

'You're bleeding...'

The fact that Rafaele's voice was rough was no comfort. He was just angry, not overcome with passion.

Sam reached up and touched her lip and winced when it stung slightly. Her mouth felt swollen. She knew she had to get out of there before he saw something. Before he saw that very close behind her anger in that exchange had been an awful yearning for something else.

'I have to go. They'll be wondering where we are.' Her insides were heaving, roiling. She was terrified she might be sick again, and this time all over Rafaele's immaculate shoes. She couldn't look at him.

'Sam—'

'No.' She cut him off and looked at him. 'Not here.'

His jaw tightened. 'Fine. I'll send a car for you this evening. We'll talk at my place.'

Sam was too much in shock to argue. Too much had happened—too much physicality. Too much of a reminder that he aroused more passion in her just by looking at him than she'd ever felt in her life with anyone else. She simply didn't have it in her right then to say anything other than a very reluctant, 'Fine.' She needed to get away from this man before he exposed her completely.

That evening, Sam waited for Rafaele in an exclusive townhouse in the middle of Mayfair, demesne of the rich and famous. Anger and an awful sense of futility had simmered in her belly all day as she'd had to put up with her colleagues excitedly discussing the great opportunity Rafaele Falcone had presented them with while knowing that it was only to ensure he gained as much control of her life as he could.

She was afraid of the volatility of her emotions after what had happened in that bathroom earlier and, worse, at the thought of working for him again. She forced herself to take deep breaths and focused on her surroundings. Luxurious sofas and chairs, dressed in shades of grey and white and cream. Low coffee tables and sleek furnishings. Seriously intimidating.

She felt very scruffy as she was still in her work uniform of narrow black trousers, white shirt and black jacket. Flat shoes. Hair pulled back. No make-up. These surroundings were made for a much more sensual woman. A woman who would drape herself seductively on a couch in a beautiful silk dress and wait for her lover.

It reminded Sam painfully of Rafaele's *palazzo* on the outskirts of Milan, where sometimes she had fooled herself into believing nothing existed beyond those four walls. And that she was one of those beautiful seductive women.

'Sorry to keep you waiting.'

Sam whirled around so abruptly when she heard his voice that she felt dizzy. She realised she was clutching her leather bag to her chest like a shield and lowered it.

She really wasn't prepared to see Rafaele again so soon, and that swirling cauldron of emotions within her was spiked with a mix of anger and ever-present shame. And the memory of that angry kiss. Her lips were still sensitive. He looked like the Devil himself, emerging from the shadows of the doorway. Tall, broad, hard, muscled. And mean. His face was harsh, his mouth unsmiling. Making a mockery of his apology for keeping her waiting.

Nothing had changed from earlier. But despite her anger Sam's conscience stung. Tightly, she said, 'I'm sorry...for hitting you earlier. I don't know what came over me...but what you said...it was wrong.'

Liar. She burned inside. She might as well have held her tongue. She was lying to herself as much as to him.

Rafaele came further in. Grim. 'I deserved it. I provoked you.'

Sam blanched and looked at him. She hadn't expected that, and somewhere treacherous a part of her melted.

He walked past her and over to a drinks board, helping himself to something amber that swirled in the bottom of a bulbous glass. He looked at her over his shoulder, making heat flood her cheeks. She hadn't even realised that she'd been making a thorough inspection of his broad back, tapering down to lean hips and firm buttocks.

'Drink?'

She shook her head hurriedly and got out a choked, 'No. Thank you.'

'Suit yourself.' He gestured to a nearby couch. 'Sit down, Sam—and you can put down your bag. You look as if your fingers might break.'

She looked down stupidly to see white knuckles through the skin of her fingers where they gripped the leather. Forcing herself to take a breath, she moved jerkily over to the couch and perched on the edge, resisting the design of it, which wanted to seduce her into a more relaxed pose.

Rafaele came and sat down opposite her, clearly far more relaxed than her as he sank back into the couch, resting one arm across the top. Sam fought the desire to look and see how his shirt must be stretched across his chest.

'What kind of a name is Milo anyway? Irish?'

Sam blinked. It took a minute for his words to sink in because they were so unexpected. 'It's...it was my grandfather's name.'

Sam was vaguely surprised he remembered that detail of her heritage. She was one generation removed from Ireland, actually, having been born and brought up in England because her parents had moved there after her brilliant father had been offered a job at a London university.

Sam sensed his anger building again. 'I did intend to tell you…some day. I would never have withheld that information from Milo for ever.'

Rafaele snorted a harsh laugh. 'That's big of you. You would have waited until he'd built up a childhood full of resentment about his absent father and I wouldn't have even known.'

Rafaele sat forward and put down his glass with a clatter. He ran his hand impatiently through his hair, making it flop messily onto his forehead. Sam's insides clenched when she remembered how she'd once felt comfortable running her hands through his hair, using it to hold him in place when he'd had his face buried between—

Shame flared inside her at the way her thoughts were going. She should be thinking of Milo and extricating them both from the threat that Rafaele posed, not remembering lurid X-rated memories.

In a smaller voice she admitted, 'I've been living day to day…it didn't seem to be urgent right now. He…he doesn't ask about his father.'

Rafaele stood up, towering over her. 'I'd say it became urgent about the time you gave birth, Sam. Don't you think he must be wondering why other kids have fathers and he doesn't?'

Words were locked in Sam's throat. Milo mightn't have mentioned anything yet, but she had noticed him looking at his friends in playschool when their fathers picked them up. It wouldn't be long before he'd start asking questions.

She stood up too, not liking feeling so intimidated.

Rafaele bit back the anger that threatened to spill over and keep spilling. Looking as vulnerable, if not more so than she had earlier, Sam said tightly, 'Look, I can't stay

too long. My minder is doing me a favour. Can we just…
get to what we need to discuss?'

He'd been unable to get Sam's pale face out of his mind
all day. Or the way he'd hauled her into his arms like a Ne-
anderthal, all but backing her up against that sink to rav-
ish her in a tacky bathroom. The feel of her against him,
under his mouth, had dragged him back to a place he'd
locked away deep inside, unleashing a cavalcade of desire
more hot and urgent than anything he'd ever encountered.

He struggled to curb some of the intense emotion he
was feeling.

'What's going to happen is this: I am going to be a father to my son and you will do everything in your power
to facilitate that—because if you don't, Samantha, I won't
hesitate to use full legal force against you.'

Rafaele delivered his ultimatum and Sam just looked
at him, trying not to let him see how his words shook her
to her core. *I won't hesitate to use full legal force against
you.*

'What exactly do you mean, Rafaele? You can't threaten
me like this.'

Rafaele came close to Sam—close enough for his scent
to wind around her, prompting a vivid memory of how it
had felt to have her mouth crushed under his earlier that
day. He looked at her for such a long, taut moment that she
stopped breathing. And then he moved back to the couch
to sit down again and regarded her like a lounging pasha.

'It's not a threat. It's very much a promise. I want to be
in Milo's life. I am his father. We deserve to get to know
one another. He needs to *know* that I am his father.'

Panic boosted Sam's adrenalin. She couldn't have sat
down if she'd wanted to. Every muscle was locked. 'You
can't just barge in and announce that you're his father. He
won't understand. It'll upset him.'

Rafaele arched a brow. 'And whose fault is that? Who

kept this knowledge from him and from me? One person, Sam. *You*. And now you have to deal with the consequences.'

'Yes,' Sam admitted bitterly, 'I recognise that, and you've already made your sphere of influence obvious—but not at the cost of my son's happiness and sense of security.'

Rafaele leant forward. 'You have cost our son his happiness and security already. You've wilfully cost him three years of knowing he had a father. You've already irreparably damaged his development.'

Our son. Sam's insides contracted painfully. She was feeling shocked again at the very evident emotion on Rafaele's face. Quickly masked, though, as if he was surprised by his own vehemence.

'So what are you proposing, Rafaele?'

A part of Sam, deep down inside, marvelled at that moment that there had ever been intimacy between them. That she had ever lain beside him in bed and gazed deep into his eyes. On their last night together…before he'd gone on his business trip…she'd reached out and touched his face as if learning every feature. He'd taken her hand and pressed a kiss to her palm, and there had been something she'd never seen before darkening his eyes, making her breath grow short and her heart pound…

'What I'm proposing is that, as I'm due to be here in England for the foreseeable future, I want to be a part of Milo's daily life so that he can get to know me.'

Sam struggled to take it in. '"The foreseeable future"? What does that mean? You can't get to know him and then just walk away, Rafaele, when your business is done.'

Rafaele stood up and put his hands deep in his pockets, as if he was having second thoughts about physical violence. Silkily he replied, 'Oh, don't worry, Sam, I have no intention of walking away—ever—no matter where my business takes me. Milo is my son just as much as he is yours. You've had unfettered access to him for over three years of his life and you will never deny me access again. I want him here—with me.'

Sam's mouth opened and closed again before she could manage to articulate, 'Here with you? But that's preposterous. He's *three!*'

Rafaele clarified with clear reluctance, 'Naturally you would also have to come.'

Sam emitted a scared laugh, because even though what Rafaele was saying was insane he sounded eminently reasonable. 'Oh, thanks! Should I be grateful that you would allow me to stay with my son?'

Rafaele's face darkened. 'I think any judge in any courtroom would look unfavourably upon a mother who kept her son from his father for no apparent good reason.'

Sam blanched and tried to appeal to him. 'Rafaele, we can't just…uproot and move in with you. It's not practical.' And the very thought of spending any more time alone with this man than she had to scared the living daylights out of her.

His voice sounded unbearably harsh. 'I am going to be under the same roof as my son, as his father, and I will not negotiate on that. You can either be part of it or not. Obviously it will be easier if you are. And, as we're going to be working together again, it can only be more practical.'

Anger surged again at Rafaele's reminder of that small detail and his intractability. 'You're being completely unreasonable. Of course I need to be with my son…*that's* non-negotiable.'

Rafaele took a step closer, and even though his hands were in his pockets Sam felt the threat reach out to touch her.

'Well, then, you have a measure of how I'm feeling, Samantha. I will expect you back here with your bags and

Milo by this time tomorrow evening or else we take it to the courts and they will decide how he will divide his time between us.' He added, 'You've proved that you believe one parent is dispensable—what's to stop me testing out the theory with you?'

Sam gritted out, 'I do recognise that you've missed out on time with Milo…and I should have told you before now. But I had my reasons and I believed they were valid.'

'Very noble of you, Samantha,' Rafaele mocked, with an edge.

Trying to concentrate and not be distracted by him, she said, 'It's just not practical for us to come here. This might be your home, and it's beautiful—'

'It's not mine,' Rafaele bit out. 'It belongs to a friend. I'm renting it.'

Sam lifted her hands in an unconscious plea for him to listen. 'All the more reason why this isn't a good idea—it's not even your permanent home. Milo is settled into a good routine where we are. We have a granny flat attached to the house and that's where Bridie lives.'

Rafaele arched a brow. 'His minder?'

Sam nodded. 'She was my father's housekeeper since I was two, after my mother died. She cared for me while I grew up and she stayed on after my father passed away two years ago.'

'I'm sorry,' Rafaele offered stiffly, 'I didn't know.'

'Thank you…' Sam acknowledged. 'The thing is,' she continued while she had Rafaele's attention, 'Bridie has known Milo since he was born. She…helped me.'

Sam coloured as she imagined the acerbic retorts going through Rafaele's mind and she rushed on. 'We have a good arrangement. Regular affordable childcare like I have is gold dust in London.'

Rafaele asserted, 'I don't think I need to point out that

affording childcare would be the least of your worries if you let me organise it.'

Sam was tense enough to crack, and all of a sudden she felt incredibly light-headed. She must have shown it, because immediately Rafaele was beside her, holding her arm and frowning.

'What is it? *Dio*, Sam, you look like death warmed up.'

His use of *Sam* caught her somewhere vulnerable. She cursed herself inwardly. She was no wilting ninny and she hated that Rafaele was seeing her like this. She pulled away from his strong grip jerkily. 'I'm fine…'

Rafaele all but forcibly manoeuvred her to the couch and made her sit down again. Then he went to the drinks cabinet and poured some brandy into a glass. Coming back, he handed it to her.

Hating herself for needing the fortification, Sam took it. She took a sip, and as the pungent and strong alcohol filtered down her throat and into her belly, felt a bit steadier. She put the glass down and looked directly at Rafaele, where he too had taken his seat again, opposite her.

'Look, you've said yourself that you're just renting this place. It would be insane to uproot Milo from the only home he's known since he was a baby.' She pressed on, 'My father's house is perfectly comfortable. Bridie lives right next door. His playschool is at the end of the road. We have a nearby park. He goes swimming at the weekends to the local pool. He plays with the children from the surrounding houses. It's a safe area. Everyone looks out for everyone and they all love Milo.'

Rafaele's face was unreadable. Sam took a breath. She'd just spoken as if in a lecture, in a series of bullet points. Never more than right now did she appreciate just how much Rafaele could upset their lives if he wanted to. And it was entirely her fault.

He drawled, 'The picture you paint is positively idyllic.'

She flushed at the sarcasm in his voice. 'We're lucky to be in a good area.'

'How have you managed financially?'

Rafaele's question blindsided Sam for a minute. 'It... well, it wasn't easy at first. I had to defer my PhD for a year. My father was ill... But I had some savings to tide us over. And he had his pension. When he died the mortgage was protected, so that was paid off. Bridie looked after Milo while I did my doctorate and I was lucky enough to be taken onto the research programme soon afterwards. We get by. We have enough.'

Unmistakable pride straightened Sam's spine. Rafaele could see it in the set of her shoulders and he had to hand it to her—grudgingly. She hadn't come running to him looking for a hand-out as soon as she'd known her pregnancy was viable. He didn't know any woman who wouldn't have taken advantage of that fact. And yet Sam had been determined to go it alone.

'Would you have come to me if you'd needed money?'

Rafaele could see her go pale at the prospect and something dark rushed to his gut. She would have preferred to struggle than to see him again. Since last Saturday's cataclysmic revelation Rafaele had been avoiding looking at the fact that he'd felt so compelled to see Sam again he'd ignored his earlier warning to himself to stay away and had gone to her house with more than a sense of anticipation in his belly. It had been something bordering much closer to a *need*. He'd tried to ignore it, but he'd been incensed that she'd been so dismissive. Uninterested.

Rafaele stood up. 'I fail to see what all this has to do with me getting what I want—which is my son.'

Sam stood up too, her cheeks flushing, making her eyes stand out like glittering pools of grey. Desire, dark and urgent, speared Rafaele.

'That's just it. You don't get it, do you? It's not about you or me. It's about Milo and what's best for *him*. He's not a pawn, Rafaele, you can't just move him around at will to get back at me. His needs must come first.'

Rafaele felt stung at her tirade. She had the right to maternal indignation because she'd experienced the bonding process. He hadn't. But he knew that she was right. He couldn't just waltz in and pluck his son out of his routine, much as he wanted to. But he hated her for this.

Tightly he asked, 'So what is your suggestion, then?'

The relief that moved across her expressive fine features made him even angrier. Did she really think it would be this easy?

'We leave Milo where he is, at home with me. And you can come and see him…we'll work something out while you're here in England…and then, once we see how it goes, we can work out a longer term arrangement. After all, you won't be here for ever…'

He could see her spying her bag nearby and she moved to get it. His eyes were drawn against his will to her tall, slim form as she bent and then straightened, her breasts pushing against her shirt, reminding him of how badly he'd ached to touch them for the first time, and what it had felt like to cup their firm weight, made perfectly to fit his palms. The fact that the memory was so vivid was not welcome.

Sam was the only woman who'd ever had this ability to make him feel slightly out of his comfort zone. Coasting on the edge of extreme danger. And not the kind he liked, where he ultimately had control, say in a car.

Danger zone or no danger zone, something primal gripped Rafaele deep inside at seeing Sam preparing to leave, looking so relieved—as if she could just lay it all on the line like this and he'd agree.

She was backing away, tucking some loose hair behind her ear, and it was that one simple familiar gesture that pushed Rafaele over an edge. 'Do you really think it's that easy? That I'll simply agree to your terms?'

She stopped. 'You can't do this, Rafaele—insist on having it your way. It's not fair on Milo. If he's going to get to know you then it should be in his own safe environment. He's going to be confused as it is.'

Rafaele moved closer to Sam, almost against his will. 'And whose fault is that?' he reminded her, as an audacious plan formed in his brain. 'What do you hope for, Sam? That after a couple of visits I'll grow bored and you'll be left in peace?'

She swallowed visibly and looked faintly guilty. 'Of course not.'

But *she did*. He could tell. She hoped that this was just a passing display of anger and might. She was probably congratulating herself on the fact that he now knew and that she and her son—*his son*—would be left in peace to get on with their lives once he'd lost interest.

Suddenly Rafaele wanted to insert himself deep into Sam's life. *Deep into her.* He remembered what that had felt like too—that moment of exquisite suspension when neither of them could draw in a breath because he was embedded so deep inside her—

'This will work *my way* or no way,' he gritted out, ruthlessly crushing those incendiary images, exerting a control over his body he rarely had to call on.

'Rafaele—'

'No, Samantha. I will concede that you are right that Milo must come first, so I agree that he should stay where he is most secure.'

'You do?'

Rafaele didn't even bother to agree again, he just continued, 'So, with that concern in mind, I will compromise.'

She swallowed again. Now she looked nervous. *Good. She should.* Rafaele smiled and got a fleeting moment of satisfaction from the way her eyes dropped to his mouth and flared with something hot.

'I'll move in with you.'

Sam's eyes met his and grew wider. He saw her struggling to compute the information. She even shook her head slightly.

'I'm sorry… I don't think I heard you properly… You said you'll what?'

Rafaele smiled even more widely now, enjoying himself for the first time in days. 'You heard me fine, Samantha, I said I'll move in with you. Then you will have no reason to deny me access to my son as I'll be doing everything in my power to accommodate you—isn't that right?'

Sam felt as if she was suspended in time, disbelieving of what she'd just heard. But then the smug look on Rafaele's face told her she hadn't misheard. *Twice.*

'But…you can't. I mean…' Her brain seemed to have turned to slush. 'There's no room.'

Rafaele quirked a brow. 'It looks like a decent-sized house to me. I would imagine there's at least three bedrooms? All I need is one.'

Sam cursed his accuracy and diverted her thoughts away from remembering Rafaele's palatial bedroom in his *palazzo*, with the bed big enough for a football team. They'd covered every inch of it.

Stiffly she said, 'It's not a good idea. You wouldn't be comfortable. It's not exactly up to this standard.' She gestured with her arm to take in the surrounding opulence.

Rafaele grimaced. 'This place is too big for just me.' And then his eyes glinted with sheer wickedness. 'I find my preferences running to much more modest requirements all of a sudden.'

Sam felt old bitterness rise. No doubt he meant much in the same way his preferences had become more 'modest' when he'd found himself briefly in thrall to her. Seduced, presumably, by her complete naivety and innocence because he'd become momentarily jaded by the far more sophisticated women he usually went for. This had been evidenced by the fact that he'd never even taken her out in too public a social setting, preferring to keep their dates secluded and *secret*.

Sam shook her head, the mere thought of Rafaele in her house for an extended period making her seize inwardly. Not to mention the fact that he expected her to work for him.

'No. This is not going to happen. Maybe if you moved closer—'

Suddenly Rafaele was far too close and Sam's words faltered. Any hint of wickedness was gone.

'No, Samantha. I am moving in with you and there is nothing you can do or say to put me off this course. I've missed important milestones already in my son's life and I'm not about to miss another moment.'

Shakily Sam said, 'Please, there must be another way to do this.'

Rafaele stepped even closer. Sam could smell him now and see the lighter flecks of green in his eyes. See the dark shadowing of stubble on his jaw. He'd always needed to shave twice a day. Her insides cramped.

'The reason you don't want me to stay, Sam... It wouldn't be because there's still something there...would it?'

Had his voice grown huskier or was it her imagination? Sam just looked at him and blinked. His eyes were molten green, hot. And she was on fire. It was only when she saw something very cynical and dark in their depths that she managed to shake herself free of his spell. She was terrified he'd touch her again, like earlier, and stepped back, feeling cold all over.

The thought that she'd given herself away, that he might

analyse her reaction and suspect that there had been something deeper there than anger made her sick with mortification and shame.

In as cool a voice as she could muster, Sam said, 'Don't be ridiculous, Rafaele. I'm no more attracted to you any more than you are to me. That died long ago.'

His eyes flashed. 'So there should be no problem with my sharing your house to facilitate me getting to know my son, who you have kept from me for the last three years?'

It wasn't really a question. Much as in the way he had ridden roughshod over her department at work, ensuring she would be under his control. With a sinking sense of inevitability Sam knew that if she fought Rafaele further he'd only dig his heels in deeper and deeper. And perhaps he'd even feel like toying with her again, proving a point, and perhaps this time she'd really give herself away.

The thought made her go clammy. She must never forget his cruel rejection or let him know how badly he'd hurt her.

She reassured herself that he was a workaholic, after all, so she'd probably barely see him. And for all his lofty talk she didn't seriously see him lasting for longer than a week in the leafy but very boring London suburbs.

A man like Rafaele—son of an Italian count and a renowned Spanish beauty—was accustomed to beautiful things and especially beautiful women. Accustomed to getting what he wanted.

Seizing on that, and also anticipating his realisation that her house would not be a haven for his mistresses and would soon bore him to tears, Sam lifted her chin and said, 'When do you propose to move in?'

CHAPTER FOUR

FOUR DAYS LATER it was Friday evening, and Sam was tense enough to crack in two, waiting for Rafaele's appearance. He was moving in tonight, and all week his staff had been arriving at the house to prepare it for his arrival.

When she'd come home from his house the previous Monday evening she'd had to come clean and tell Bridie what had happened. The older woman had reacted with admirable nonchalance.

'He's his father, you say?'

'Yes,' Sam had replied, *sotto voce*, giving Bridie a look to tell her to be mindful of small ears nearby as Milo had been in the sitting room, watching a cartoon before bed.

Unfortunately Bridie had been enjoying this revelation far too much. She'd taken a sip of tea and then repeated, 'His father... Well, I never, Sam. You're a dark one, aren't you? I always thought it might have been a waiter or a mechanic at the factory or something...but it's actually himself—the Falcone boss...'

Sam had gritted out, 'He's only moving in temporarily. He'll be bored within a week, believe me.'

Bridie had sniffed disapprovingly. 'Well, let's hope not for Milo's sake.'

Sam's hands stilled under the water now, as she washed the dinner dishes. She could hear Milo's chatter to Bridie nearby. She was doing this for him. She had to stop thinking about herself and think of him. It was the only way she'd get through this, because if she focused for a second on what it meant for her to be thrown into such close proximity with Rafaele again she felt the urgent compulsion to run fast and far away.

Bridie bustled into the kitchen then, and Sam noticed her badly disguised expression of anticipation. She might have smiled if she'd been able.

'You really don't have to wait till he gets here.'

The housekeeper smiled at her sunnily and started drying dishes. 'Oh, I wouldn't miss this for the world, Sam. It's better than the Pope's visit to Dublin back in the seventies.'

Suddenly the low, powerful throb of an engine became obvious outside. To Sam's chagrin she found that she was automatically trying to analyse the nuances of the sound, figuring out the components of the engine.

Milo's ears must have pricked up, because he came into the kitchen excitedly and announced, 'Car!'

They didn't have a car themselves, much to his constant disappointment, and Sam couldn't stop him running towards the door now. When the bell rang her palms grew sweaty. Before she could move, though, Bridie was beating her to it, and Sam only noticed then that Bridie, who never wore an apron, had put one on. She wanted to roll her eyes.

But then the door opened and Sam's world condensed down to the tall dark figure filling the frame against the dusky evening. She hadn't seen him since Monday and she hated the way her heart leapt in her chest.

Milo said with some surprise from beside Bridie, 'It's the man.' And then, completely oblivious to the atmosphere, 'Do you have a car?'

Rafaele's gaze had zeroed in immediately on Sam, and she was glad now that she had the buffer of Bridie at the door. Bridie was doing her thing now, extending her hand, introducing herself, practically twinkling with Irish charm.

Lots of *'sure'* and *'Won't you come in out of that cold?'*. Ridiculously, Sam felt betrayed.

Rafaele stepped in and Sam's chest constricted. He looked so alien, foreign. Too gorgeous for this environment. Finally she found her legs and moved forward to pick Milo up. His eyes were huge as he took Rafaele in, again.

Milo repeated his question. 'Do you have a car, mister?'

Rafaele looked at Milo and Sam could see how his cheeks flared with colour. His eyes took on a glow that she'd never seen before…or maybe she thought she had… once. Her arms tightened fractionally around Milo. Bridie had bustled off somewhere, saying something about tea and coffee. Now it was just the three of them.

His voice was so deep it resonated within Sam.

'Yes, I do have a car… I'm Rafaele…and what's your name?'

The fact that Rafaele's voice had gone husky made Sam's guilt rush to the fore again. Milo buried his head in Sam's neck, his little arms tight around her neck.

She said to Milo's obscured face, 'Don't you remember me telling you that Mr Falcone would be moving in to live with us for a while?' Milo nodded against her neck, still hiding. She looked back at Rafaele. 'He's just a bit shy with strangers at first.'

Rafaele's eyes flashed dangerously at that reminder of his status and Sam said quickly, 'You can leave your jacket and things in the hall.'

He started to divest himself of his expensive black coat, revealing a dark suit underneath. Bridie reappeared then, unusually pink in the cheeks, and took Milo from Sam's arms, saying, 'I think it's bedtime for someone…there's refreshments in the drawing room.'

Sam wanted to roll her eyes again. Since when had Bridie referred to the main reception room as *the drawing room*? Or said *refreshments*? Or got pink in the cheeks from preparing tea?

She called after them. 'I'll be up to read a story in a little while.'

All she could hear, though, was Milo's plaintive, 'I want to see the car,' and Bridie reassuring him briskly that he could see it in the morning if he was a good boy and brushed his teeth before bed.

Hating Rafaele right then, for imposing himself on them like this and upsetting their equilibrium, Sam forced herself to look at him and bit out, 'I'll give you a tour, shall I?'

Rafaele smiled, but it didn't reach his eyes. 'That would be lovely.'

As perfunctorily as she could, while uncomfortably aware of Rafaele breathing down her neck, Sam showed him around the ground floor of the house.

He stopped in the study and took in the impressive array of equipment set up for his benefit, surprising her by saying, 'This was your father's study?'

'Yes,' Sam answered, more huskily than she would have liked, caught by a sudden upsurge of emotion at remembering her scatty, absent-minded father spending hours on end in here, oblivious to everything. Her chest tightened. *Oblivious to his daughter.*

'They should not have set up in here…it's not appropriate.'

Sam looked at Rafaele, surprised by this assertion. By this evidence of sensitivity.

'No…it's fine. It's been lying empty. It should be used.' Her mouth twisted wryly. 'Believe me, you could have set all this up here while he was still alive and he wouldn't have even noticed.'

Feeling exposed under Rafaele's incisive green gaze, Sam backed out of the room.

'Upstairs. I'll show you your room.'

She hurried up the stairs, very aware of Rafaele behind her, conscious of her drab work uniform. Again.

She opened and closed doors with almost indecent speed, and they passed where Milo was chattering nineteen to the dozen with Bridie as she helped him brush his teeth in the bathroom, standing on a little box so he could reach the sink.

Rafaele stopped outside for a long moment, and when he finally turned to keep following Sam she shivered at the look of censure in his eyes. That brief moment of sensitivity had evidently passed.

When she didn't open the door to her bedroom, but just gestured at it with clear reluctance, Rafaele pushed past her and opened the door. He looked in for a long moment, before slanting her an unmistakably mocking look. She burned inside with humiliation and hated to imagine what he must think of the room. It hadn't been redecorated since she'd left home for college and still sported dusky pink rose wallpaper.

The faded décor now seemed to scream out her innermost teenage fantasies of *not* being the school nerd, of her deeply secret wish to be just like all the other girls. No wonder Rafaele had seduced her so easily. He'd unwittingly tapped into the closet feminine romantic that Sam had repressed her whole life in a bid to be accepted by her father, turning herself into a studious tomboy.

Aghast to be thinking of this now, she swallowed her mortification, reached past Rafaele and pulled the door firmly closed in his face. Then she led him to his room.

Thankfully it was at the other end of the house from her room and Milo's, which was opposite hers. And, even better, it had an *en suite* bathroom. After that cataclysmic moment in the university the other day she had no intention of running into a half-naked Rafaele on his way to the bathroom.

Rafaele barely gave the room a cursory once-over. As she led him back downstairs Sam sent up another silent prayer that he was already chafing to get back to his own rarefied world, where his every whim was indulged before he'd even articulated it out loud.

Bridie had indeed set out tea and coffee in the front room. Sam poured coffee and handed it to him, watching warily as he sat down on the comfy but decidedly thread-bare sofa.

He looked around, taking in the homely furnishings. 'You have a nice house.'

Sam took a seat as far away from Rafaele as possible. She all but snorted. 'Hardly what you're used to.'

He levelled her a look that would have sent his minions running. 'I'm not a snob, Samantha. I may have had a priv-ileged upbringing, but when I set out to resurrect Falcone Industries I had nothing but the shirt on my back. I lived in an apartment the size of your porch and worked three jobs to put myself through college.'

Sam frowned, a little blindsided by this revelation. 'But your stepfather—he was a Greek billionaire…'

Rafaele's mouth twisted. 'Who hated my guts because I wasn't his son. The only reason he put me through school at all was because of my mother. He washed his hands of me as soon as he could and I paid him back every cent he'd doled out for my education.'

He'd never told her this before—had always shied away from talking about personal things. She'd always assumed that he'd been given a hand-out to restart Falcone Indus-tries. It was one of the most well-documented resurrections of a company in recent times. Spectacular in its success. She recalled his mother ringing from time to time, and their clipped conversations largely conducted in Spanish, which was her first language.

At a loss to know what to say, Sam went for the easiest thing. 'How *is* your mother?'

Rafaele's face tightened almost imperceptibly but Sam noticed.

'She died three months ago. A heart attack.'

'I'm sorry, Rafaele,' Sam responded. 'I had no idea...' She gestured helplessly. 'I must have missed it in the papers.'

His Spanish mother had been a world-renowned beauty and feted model. Her marriages and lovers had been well documented. The rumour was that she had cruelly left Rafaele's father when it had become apparent that he'd lost everything except his title. But this was only hearsay that Sam had picked up when she'd gone to Milan to work for Falcone Industries as an intern.

Rafaele shook his head, his mouth thin. 'It was overshadowed by the economic crisis in Greece so it barely made the papers—something we welcomed.'

Sam could remember how much Rafaele had hated press intrusion and the constant glare of the paparazzi lens. He put down his cup and stood abruptly. Sam looked up, her breath sticking in her throat for a minute as he loomed so large and intimidating. *Gorgeous*. Lord, how was she going to get through even twenty-four hours of him living under the same roof, just down the hall? Did he still sleep naked—?

'...will you tell him?'

Sam flushed hotly when she registered Rafaele looking at her expectantly. He'd just asked her a question and she'd been so busy speculating on whether or not he still slept naked that she hadn't heard him.

She stood up so quickly her knees banged against the coffee table and she winced. 'Tell who what?'

Rafaele looked irritated. 'When are you going to tell Milo that I am his father?'

Sam crossed her arms over breasts that felt heavy and tingly. 'I think…I think when he's got used to you being here. When he's got to know you a bit…then we can tell him.' She cursed herself for once again proving that her mind was all too easily swayed by this man.

He nodded. 'I think that's fair enough.'

Sam breathed out, struck somewhere vulnerable at seeing Rafaele intent on putting Milo's needs first, over his wish to punish her.

Just then Bridie put her head around the door. 'I'm off, love, and Milo is waiting for his story. If you need me over the weekend just call me. Nice to meet you, Mr Falcone.'

Sam moved towards the door, more in a bid to get away from Rafaele than a desire to see Bridie out, but the older woman waved her back with a definite glint in her eyes.

'Stay where you are.'

Rafaele murmured goodnight and then Bridie was gone. Sam heard the sound of the front door opening and closing. And now she really was alone in the house with the man she'd hoped never to see again and her son. *Milo.* The incongruity of Rafaele Falcone, international billionaire and playboy, here in her suburban house, was overwhelming to say the least.

She backed towards the door. 'I should go to Milo. He'll come looking for me if I don't.' Why did she suddenly sound as if she'd just been running?

Rafaele inclined his head. 'I have some work to attend to, if you don't mind me using the study?'

Sam was relieved at the prospect of some space. 'Of course not.'

And then she fled, taking the stairs two at a time as she had when she'd been a teenager.

Rafaele heard Sam take the stairs at a gallop and shook his head. He looked around the room again. Definitely not the milieu he was accustomed to, in spite of his defence to

Sam. Those gruelling years when he'd done nothing but work, study, sleep and repeat were a blur now.

He felt slightly shell-shocked at how easily he'd told Sam something he never discussed. It was no secret that he'd turned his back on his stepfather to resurrect his family legacy, but people invariably drew their own conclusions.

His mouth tightened. He'd resisted the urge to spill his guts before—had been content to distract them both from talking by concentrating on the physical. Avoiding a deeper intimacy at all costs.

Rafaele cursed and ran his hands through his hair, feeling constricted in his suit. He'd come straight here from a meeting in town. As soon as he'd walked in through the front door he'd felt the house closing in around him claustrophobically and he'd had a bizarre urge to turn on his heel, get back into his car and drive very fast in the opposite direction.

For a wild few seconds when he'd looked at Sam waiting in the hall the only thing he'd been able to remember was how he'd all but devoured her only days before. He'd assured himself that he could just send in his lawyers and have her dictated to, punished for not telling him about Milo.

But then he'd seen Milo, held in her arms, and the claustrophobia had disappeared. *That* was why he was here. Because he didn't want more months to go by before he got a chance to let his son know who he was. More months added on top of the three years he'd already missed. Rafaele had never really forgiven his own father for falling apart and checking out of his life so spectacularly. For investing so much in a woman who had never loved him. For allowing himself to turn into something maudlin and useless.

For years Rafaele had been jealous of his younger

brother, Alexio, who had grown up bathed in his father's love and support. So much so, however, that Rafaele knew how stifling Alexio had found it, prompting him to turn his back on his own inheritance. He smiled grimly to himself. Maybe that just proved one could never be happy?

He made his way to the study and sat down behind the desk, firing up various machines. He stopped abruptly when he heard movement above his head. His heart twisted at the realisation that he must be underneath Milo's room. Obeying an urge he couldn't ignore, Rafaele stood up and walked out of the room and up the stairs, as silent as a panther.

He saw the half-open door of Milo's room and stopped when he could see inside. The scene made him suck in a breath. Sam was leaning back against a headboard painted in bright colours with Milo in her embrace. She held a book open in front of them and was reading aloud, putting on funny voices, making Milo giggle.

Rafaele had forgotten that she wore glasses to read and write. They made her look seriously studious, but also seriously sexy. Her mouth was plump and pink. Even in the plain white shirt and trousers her slim curves were evident. This sight of her was hugely disconcerting. He'd never expected to see her in this situation. And yet something about it called to him—an echo of an emotion he'd crushed ruthlessly when she'd first told him she was pregnant. Before the shock had hit, and the cynical suspicion that she'd planned it, had come something far more disturbing. Something fragile and alien.

He hated her right then for still having an effect on him. For still making him want her. For invading his imagination when he'd least expected it over the last four years. He would find it hard to recall his last lover's name right now, but Sam...her name had always been indelible. And this was utterly galling when she'd proved to be as treacherous as his own mother in her own way. When she'd kept the most precious thing from him. His son.

For a moment Rafaele questioned his sanity in deciding to take over funding the research programme at the university in a bid to get to Sam. But then he remembered looking down into Milo's green eyes and recognising his own DNA like a beacon winking back at him.

As much as there was a valid reason behind his rationale, it had also come from that deeper place not linked solely to rationale and he hated to admit that.

His eyes went to his son and Rafaele put a hand to his chest, where an ache was forming. He would make it his life's mission to keep Sam from sidelining him from his own son's life. Whatever it took. Even if it meant spending twenty-four hours a day with her. He could resist her. How could he desire a woman who had denied him his most basic right of all? His own flesh and blood.

Later, when Sam was in bed, the familiar creakings of the old house which normally comforted her sounded sinister. Rafaele Falcone was separated from her only by some bricks and mortar. And reality was slowly sinking in. Her new reality. Living and working with Rafaele Falcone. She suspected that he'd flexed his muscles to get her to work for him as much to irritate her as for any *bona fide* professional reason, even if that was why he'd first contacted her.

The thought of going back into that factory environment made her feel clammy. Although she'd loved it the first time around—it had been so exciting, getting an internship with one of the most innovative and successful motor companies in the world.

Rafaele had made his initial fortune by devising a computer software program which aided in the design of cars, and that was how he'd first come onto the scene, stunning the world with its success. That was how he'd been able to fund getting Falcone Motors off the ground again—injecting it with new life, turning around the perception of the Falcone car as outdated and prehistoric. Now Falcone cars were the most coveted on the race track *and* on the roads.

And Sam had been in the thick of it, working on new cutting edge designs, figuring out the most fuel-efficient engine systems. From her very first day, though, she'd been aware of Rafaele. She'd gone bright red whenever she saw him, never expecting him to be as gorgeous in the flesh as he was in press photos.

He'd surprised her by being very hands-on, not afraid to get dirty himself, and invariably he knew more than all of them put together, displaying an awesome intelligence and intellect. And, in a notoriously male-dominated industry, she'd met more females working in his factory than she'd encountered in all her years as a student. Clearly when he said equal opportunities he meant it.

Sam had found that each day she was seeking him out… only to look away like a naive schoolgirl if he met her gaze, which he'd appeared to do more and more often. She'd been innocent—literally. A childhood spent with an emotionally distant father and with her head buried in books hadn't made for a well-rounded adolescence. While her peers had been experimenting with boys Sam had been trying in vain to connect with her scatty but brilliant father. Bridie had been in despair, and had all but given up encouraging Sam to get out and enjoy herself, not to worry so much about studying or her father.

The irony of it all was that while the more predominantly masculine areas *did* appeal to her—hence her subsequent career—she'd always longed to feel more feminine. And it was this very secret desire that Rafaele had unwittingly tapped into so effectively. Just by looking at her, he had made Sam feel like a woman for the first time in her life.

One of their first conversations had been over an intricate engine. The other interns and engineers had walked away momentarily and Sam had been about to follow them when Rafaele had caught her wrist. He'd let her go again almost immediately but her skin had burned for hours afterwards, along with the fire in her belly.

'So,' he'd drawled in that sexy voice, 'where did your interest and love for engines come from, Miss Rourke?'

The *Miss Rourke* had sounded gently mocking, as if some sort of secret code had passed between them. Sam had been mesmerised and it had taken a second for her to answer. She'd shrugged, looking away from the penetrating gaze that had seemed to see her in a way that was both exhilarating and terrifying.

'My father is a professor of physics, so I've grown up surrounded by science. And my grandmother…his mother…she was Irish, but she ended up in England during the Second World War, working in the factories on cars. Apparently she loved it and had a natural affinity for working with engines—so much so that she kept her job after the war for a few years, before returning home to marry.' She'd shrugged again. 'I guess it ran in the family.'

Sam looked back at her young naive self now and cringed. She'd been so transparent, so easy to seduce. It had taken one earth-shattering kiss in Rafaele's office and she'd opened herself up for him, had forgotten everything her upbringing had taught her about protecting herself from emotionally unavailable people.

He'd whispered to her that she was sensual, sexy, beautiful, and she'd melted. A girl who had grown up denying her very sexuality had had no defence mechanism in place to deal with someone as practised and polished and seductive as Rafaele.

She'd fallen for him quicker than Alice in Wonderland had fallen down the rabbit hole. And her world had changed as utterly as Alice's: beautiful dresses, intoxicating dates—one night he'd even flown them to Venice in his helicopter for dinner.

And then there had been the sex. He'd taken her innocence with a tenderness she never would have expected of a consummate seducer. It had been mind-blowing, addictive. Almost overwhelming for Sam, who had never imagined her boring, almost boyish body could arouse someone— never mind a man like Rafaele Falcone, who had his pick of the world's most beautiful women.

During their short-lived affair, even though he'd told her, 'Samantha…don't fall for me. Don't hope for something more because I have nothing to give someone like you…' she hadn't listened. She'd told herself that he had to feel *something*, because when they made love it felt as if they transcended everything that bound them to this earth and touched something profound.

At the time, though, she'd laughed and said airily, belying her own naivety, 'Relax, Rafaele! It is possible, you know, for not every woman you meet to fall in love with you. I know what this is. It's just sex.'

She'd made herself say it out loud, even though it had been like turning a knife towards her own belly and thrusting it deep. Because she'd been so far out of her depth by then she might as well have been in the middle of the Atlantic Ocean. She'd been lying, of course. She'd proved to be as humiliatingly susceptible to Rafaele's lethal charm as the next hapless woman.

If anything, he'd given her a life lesson and a half. For a brief moment she'd lost her head and forgotten that if it looked like a dream and felt like a dream, then it probably was a dream. Her real world was far more banal and she'd always been destined to return to it. Milo or no Milo.

Punching the pillow beneath her head now, as if she could punch the memories away too, Sam closed her eyes

and promised herself that not for a second would she ever
betray just how badly that man had hurt her.

'Mummy, the man is still here. He's downstairs in the
book room.'

Sam responded to the none-too-gentle shaking of her
son and opened her eyes. She'd finally fallen asleep somewhere around dawn. *Again.* Milo's eyes were huge in his
face and Sam struggled to sit up, pulling him into her, feeling her stomach clench at the reminder of who was here.

'I told you that he'd be moving in with us for a while,
don't you remember?' she prompted sleepily.

Milo nodded and then asked, 'But where's *his* house?'

Sam smiled wryly. Little did her son know that his father had a veritable portfolio of houses around the world.

'He doesn't have a house here in London.'

'Okay.' Milo clambered out of the bed and looked at her
winsomely. 'Can we get Cheerios now?'

Sam got out of bed and reached for her robe—and then
thought better of it when she imagined Rafaele giving its
threadbare appearance a caustic once-over. No doubt he
would wonder what on earth he'd ever seen in her.

Hating to be so influenced by what he might think,
Sam reached for jeans and a thin sweatshirt and yanked
her sleep-mussed hair into a ponytail. No make-up. She
cursed herself. She wasn't trying to seduce Rafaele, for
crying out loud.

Milo was jumping around now and then stopped. 'Do
you…do you think he'll eat Cheerios too?' He looked comically stricken. 'What if he eats *my* Cheerios?'

Sam bent down and tweaked Milo's nose. 'He won't
touch your Cheerios while I'm around. Anyway, I happen
to know for a fact that he only likes coffee for breakfast.'

Something poignant gripped her as she remembered

lazy mornings when Rafaele would take great pleasure in feeding her but not himself, much to her amusement.

'Ugh,' declared Milo, already setting off out of the room, 'Coffee is *yuck*.'

Sam heard him go downstairs, sounding like a herd of baby elephants, and took a deep breath before following him. The study door was ajar, and as she passed she could hear the low deep tones that had an instant effect on her insides.

Milo was pointing with his finger and saying in a very loud stage whisper, 'He's in there.'

Sam just nodded and put a finger to her lips, then herded Milo towards the kitchen, where he quickly got distracted helping to set the table.

And even though she knew Rafaele was in the house she still wasn't prepared when she turned around and saw him standing in the doorway, looking dark and gorgeous in faded jeans and a thin jumper. It did little to disguise the inherent strength of his very powerful masculine form, akin to that of an athlete. He was so *sexy*. With that unmistakable foreign edge that no English man could ever hope to pull off.

The memory of his initial effect on her four years ago was still raw, but she forced herself to say civilly, 'Good morning. I hope you slept well?'

He smiled faintly but she noticed it barely touched those luminous green eyes. 'Like a log.'

Milo piped up, 'That's silly. *Logs* can't sleep.'

Rafaele looked at his son and again Sam noticed the way something in his face and eyes softened. He came into the kitchen and sat down at the table near Milo. 'Oh, really? What should I say, then?'

Milo was embarrassed now with the attention and started squirming in his chair. 'Aunty Bridie says she sleeps like a baby, and babies sleep all the time.'

'Okay,' Rafaele said. 'I slept like a baby. Is that right?'

Milo was still embarrassed and avoided Rafaele's eyes, but then curiosity got the better of him and he squinted him a look. 'You sound funny.'

Rafaele smiled. 'That's because I come from a place called Italy...so I speak Italian. That's why I sound funny.'

Milo looked at Sam. 'Mummy, how come we don't sound like the man?'

Sam avoided Rafaele's eyes. She put Milo's bowl of cereal down in front of him and chided gently, 'His name is Rafaele.' And then, 'Because we come from England and we speak English. To some people *we* would sound funny.'

But Milo was already engrossed in his food, oblivious to the undercurrents between the two adults in the small kitchen. Sam risked a glance at Rafaele and blanched. His look said it all: *The reason he thinks I sound funny is because you've denied him his heritage.*

Sam turned to the coffee machine as if it was the most interesting thing on the planet and said, too brightly, 'Would you like some coffee?'

She heard a chair scrape and looked around to see Rafaele standing up. 'I had some earlier. I have to go to the factory for a while today but I'll be back later. Don't worry about dinner or anything like that—I have to go out tonight to a function.'

'Oh.' Sam rested her hands on the counter behind her. She hated the sudden deflated feeling in her solar plexus. But hadn't she expected this? So why was she feeling disappointed? And angry?

The words spilled out before she could stop them. 'I forgot that weekends for you are just as important as any other day.' *Except for when he'd spent that whole last weekend in bed with her, and diverted his phone calls.*

Rafaele's eyes flashed. 'We're taking in delivery of some specially manufactured parts today and I need to make sure they're up to spec because we start putting them into new cars next week. Something,' he drawled, with that light of triumph in his eyes, '*you'll* be dealing with next week when you come to work.'

Sam's insides clenched hard even as a treacherous flicker of interest caught her. She'd forgotten for a moment.

Before she could respond, Rafaele had dismissed her and was bending down to Milo's eye level. His ears had inevitably pricked up at the mention of cars. 'I was thinking that maybe tomorrow you'd like to come for a drive in my car?'

Milo's eyes lit up and he immediately looked at Sam with such a pleading expression that she would have had to be made of stone to resist.

'Okay…*if* Rafaele still feels like it tomorrow. He might be tired, though, or—'

He cut her off with ice in his voice. 'I won't be tired.'

'But you're going out tonight,' Sam reminded him.

Immediately her head was filled with visions of Rafaele and some blonde—of him creeping back into the house like a recalcitrant student at dawn, dishevelled and with stubble lining his jaw.

But he was shaking his head and the look in his eye was mocking, as if he could read her shameful thoughts. 'I won't be tired,' he repeated.

He was walking out of the kitchen when Sam thought of something and followed him. He looked back at her as he put on his leather coat and she held out a key. 'The spare front door key.'

He came and reached for it and their fingers touched. A sizzle of electricity shot up Sam's arm and she snatched her hand back as if burnt, causing the key to drop to the ground. Cheeks burning with humiliation, she bent and picked it up before Rafaele could and handed it to him again, avoiding his eye.

And then, to her everlasting relief, he was out of the door. She turned around and breathed in deep, barely aware of Milo running to the reception room window so he could see the car pull away. She had to get a hold of herself around this man or she'd be a quivering wreck by the end of a week.

CHAPTER FIVE

WHEN SAM HEARD the telltale purr of a powerful engine as she lay in bed that night she looked at her clock in disbelief. It was before midnight and Rafaele was home? *Home.* She grimaced at how easily that had slipped into her mind.

Feeling like a teenager, but unable to help herself, she got out of bed and went to her window, pulling back the curtain ever so slightly. Her heart was thumping. Rafaele hadn't got out of the car yet, and even from here she could see his hands gripping the steering wheel tightly.

Sam had the uncanny feeling that he was imagining the wheel was her neck. Then suddenly the door opened and he got out, unfolding his huge frame from the sleek low-slung vehicle. In any other instance Sam would have sighed in sheer awe at the stunningly designed lines.

She stopped breathing as she took in Rafaele, just standing there for a moment. He wore a tuxedo. Sam knew from past experience that he had a dressing room and fully stocked wardrobe at his office. His shirt was open at the throat, his bow tie hanging rakishly undone.

Rafaele shut the car door and then surprised her by leaning back against the car and putting his hands deep in his pockets, crossing his long legs at the ankle. He looked down, and something about him was so intensely *lonely* that Sam felt like a voyeur. She hated the way her heart clenched.

She'd been so stunned to see him again that she hadn't really contemplated how much of a shock it must have been for him discovering he had a son. He would never forgive her.

Sam quickly shut the curtain again and climbed back into bed, feeling cold from the inside. Eventually she heard the opening and closing of the front door, and then heavy footsteps. She held her breath for a moment when she fancied they stopped outside her door, and then, when she heard the faintest sounds of another door closing, let her breath out in a shuddery whoosh.

About an hour later Sam gave up any pretence of trying to sleep. She threw back the covers and padded softly out of her bedroom. All was quiet and still. She looked in on Milo, who was sprawled across his bed fast asleep, and then made her way to the kitchen to get some water. She was halfway into the room before she realised she wasn't alone.

She gave a small yelp of shock when she saw Rafaele in the corner of the kitchen, in low-slung faded jeans, bare feet and a T-shirt, calmly lifting a coffee cup to his lips.

She put a hand to her rapid heart. 'You scared me. I thought you were in bed.'

Rafaele arched a brow mockingly. 'Don't tell me—you couldn't sleep until you knew I was home safe?'

Sam scowled and hated that he'd caught her like this: sleep-mussed, wearing nothing but brief pants and a threadbare V-necked T-shirt.

Anger rushed through her. Anger at the day she'd spent with her thoughts revolving sickeningly around one person—*him*. Anger that she had to face him like this in what she would have once considered her sanctuary. And, worst of all, anger at herself for not having told him about Milo when she should have.

Feeling emotional, and terrified he'd see it, she stalked

to the sink. 'I'm just getting some water. I couldn't sleep and it has nothing to do with you coming home or not.'

Liar.

Sam heard his voice over the gush of water.

'I couldn't sleep either.'

Sam remembered the intensely lonely air about him as he'd waited outside before coming in. Now she felt guilty for having witnessed it. She held the glass of water in both hands and turned, feeling disorientated.

She looked at the coffee cup and remarked dryly, 'Well, that's hardly likely to help matters.'

Rafaele shrugged and drained the coffee, the strong column of his throat working. He put the cup down. 'When I couldn't sleep I came down to do some work.'

His gaze narrowed on her then, and Sam's skin prickled. She gripped the glass tighter.

He drawled, 'But as I'm just a guest in your house perhaps I should ask for permission?'

Sam's anger was back just like that. Anger at herself for thinking she'd seen Rafaele vulnerable even for a moment. 'But you're not really a guest, are you? You're here to punish me, to make me pay for not telling you about your son.'

Feeling agitated, Sam put down the glass, sloshing some water over the side. She clenched her hands and rounded on Rafaele. 'I'm sorry, okay? I'm sorry that I didn't tell you about Milo. I should have, and I didn't. And I'm sorry.'

Rafaele went very still and put his hands in his pockets. The air thickened between them and swirled with electricity. He looked relaxed, but Sam could tell he was as tense as she was.

'Why?'

One word, a simple question, and Sam felt something crumble inside her. He hadn't actually asked her that yet. He'd asked her *how* she could have, but not why.

She looked down and put her arms around herself in an

unconscious gesture of defence, unaware of how it pushed her breasts up and unaware of how Rafaele's eyes dropped there for a moment or the flush that darkened his cheekbones. She was only aware of her own inner turmoil. She would never be brave enough to tell him of her hurt and her own secret suspicion that it had been that weak emotion that had been her main motivator. She was too ashamed.

She steeled herself and looked up. Rafaele's eyes glittered in the gloom. 'It was for all the reasons I've already told you, Rafaele. I was in shock. I'd almost lost my baby only days after finding out that I was pregnant in the first place. It was all…too much. And I truly believed you had no interest—that you would prefer if I just went away and didn't bother you again.'

She almost quailed at the way his jaw tightened but went on. 'My father was not really there for me. Ever. Even though he brought me up and we lived in this house together. He didn't know how to relate to me. What I needed. I think…I thought I was doing the right thing by keeping Milo from a similar experience.'

Rafaele crossed his arms too, making his muscles bunch. It felt as if something was fizzing between them under the words. A subtext that was alive. All she could see was that powerful body. Lean and hard.

'You had no right.'

Sam looked at him, willing down the way her body insisted on being divorced from her mind, becoming aroused as if nothing had happened between them. As if he didn't hate her.

'I know,' she said flatly. 'But it happened, and you're going to have to let it go or Milo will pick up on it—especially now you're living here too.'

Anger surged within Rafaele at her pronouncement. He uncrossed his arms, unable to disguise his frustration. Sam was standing before him, and despite the charged atmosphere and the words between them he was acutely aware that all he wanted to do was rip that flimsy T-shirt over her head and position her on the counter behind her so that he could thrust deep into her and obliterate all the questions and turmoil in his head.

When she'd walked into the room all he'd seen had been the tantalising shape of her firm breasts, their pointed tips visible through the thin fabric. Her sleep-mussed hair had reminded him of when she'd been on top of him, riding him, her head falling back...

Desire was like a wild thing inside him, clawing for fulfilment. It wasn't helped by the fact that in a bid to prove that Sam *didn't* have this unique effect on him, he'd found himself hitting on his friend's mistress at the function earlier. Flirting with her, handing her his card—desperate to provoke some response in his flatlining libido. He'd acted completely out of character, managed to insult his friend Andreas Xenakis, and he'd proved nothing.

Except that he wanted this woman more than ever.

He hated her. But he wanted her. And he wanted his son.

'Let it go?' he asked now with deceptive softness, and something in him exulted when he saw how Sam paled slightly. 'I think I've more than proved myself to be accommodating where my son and your deception are concerned.'

Rafaele knew he was reacting to Sam's almost patronising tone and to his anger at this inconvenient desire.

His lip curled. 'Do you really think I would be here in the suburbs with you if it wasn't in my son's best interests? Do you really think I want you working at the factory for any reason other than because I want to keep you where I can see your every treacherous move?'

She paled even more at that, and Rafaele felt something lance him deep inside, but he couldn't stop.

'You've put us all in this position by choosing the path

that you did. By believing that you knew best. Well, now I know best and you're just going to have to live with it. *You're* going to have to let it go, Samantha.'

The hurt Sam felt at Rafaele's words shamed her. He looked as hard and obdurate as a granite block just feet away. And as unyielding. The thought of them ever reaching some sort of amicable agreement felt like the biggest and most ludicrous fantasy on earth. And yet between her legs her panties chafed uncomfortably against swollen slick folds of flesh. She wanted to scream out her frustration at her wayward body.

Just before he'd fallen asleep earlier Milo had asked, in a small, hesitant voice, 'Will the man…I mean Rafelli… will he remember to take me in the car tomorrow?'

Anger at Rafaele's assertion that he was doing his utmost to think of Milo when all he seemed to be concerned about was needling her made her lash out. 'You might feel like you're sacrificing your glamorous life for your son, Rafaele, but when will you get bored and want out? Milo has been talking about you all day. He's terrified you won't remember to take him out in the car tomorrow. He's fast heading for hero-worship territory and he'll be devastated if you keep leading him on this path only to disappear from his life.'

Sam was breathing heavily. 'This is what I wanted to avoid all along. Milo's vulnerable. He doesn't understand what's going on between us. You can punish me all you want, Rafaele, but it's Milo who matters now. And I can't say sorry again.'

Rafaele was completely unreadable, but Sam sensed his tension spike.

'What makes you think that I am going to disappear from Milo's life?'

The words were softly delivered, but Sam could sense the volcanic anger behind them.

'You know what I mean. You're not going to stay here for ever. You'll leave sooner or later. Milo will be confused. Upset.'

Sam was aware that she could have been talking about herself, about what had happened to her.

Panic at the way Rafaele took a step closer made Sam's breath choppy. Instinctively she moved back. 'I think this was a very bad idea. I think you should move out before he gets too attached. You can visit us. That way he won't be so upset when you leave...we'll have proper boundaries.'

'Boundaries, you say?' His accent sounded thicker. 'Like the kind of boundaries you put around yourself and my son when you decided that it would be a good idea not to inform me of his existence?'

'You're just...not about commitment, Rafaele. You said it yourself to me over and over again. And a child is all about commitment—a lifetime of it.'

Rafaele was so close now that she could see veritable sparks shooting from those green depths.

His voice was low and blistering. 'How dare you patronise me? You have had the experience of giving birth to a baby and all the natural bonding that goes with it—a bonding experience *you* decided to deny me. I now have the task of bonding with my son when his personality is practically formed. He has missed out on the natural bonding between a father and son. You have deprived us both of that.'

He stopped in front of her and Sam found it hard to concentrate when she could smell his musky heat. The anger within her was vying with something far hotter and more dangerous.

'I can give my son a lifetime of commitment. That is not a problem. If and when I do leave this place he will know I am his father. He will be as much a part of me and my life as the very air I breathe.'

His eyes pinned her to the spot.

'Know this, Sam. I am in Milo's life now, and yours, and I'm not going away. I am his father and I am not shirking that responsibility. You and I are going to have to learn to co-exist.'

Sam's arms were so tight now that she felt she might be constricting the bloodflow to her brain. 'I'm willing to try to co-exist, Rafaele. But sooner or later you'll have to forgive me, or we'll never move on.'

Rafaele stood for a long moment after Sam had left, his heart still racing. She had no idea how close he'd come to reaching for her, pulling her into him so that he could taste her again.

Sooner or later you'll have to forgive me.

For the first time Rafaele didn't feel the intense anger surge. Instead he thought of Sam's stricken pale features that day in the clinic. He remembered his own sense of panic, and the awful shameful relief when he could run away, far and fast, and put Sam and the emotions she'd evoked within him behind him.

For the first time he had to ask the question: if he'd been in her position would he have done the same thing? If he'd believed that his baby was unwanted by one parent? It wasn't so black and white any more. Rafaele had to admit to the role he'd played.

Completely unbidden a memory came to him of something Sam had told him one night while they'd been lying in bed. It was something he avoided like the plague—the post-coital intimacy that women seemed engineered to pursue—but this hadn't been like that. Sam had started telling him something and then stopped. He'd urged her on.

It was her mention of her relationship with her father just a short while before that had brought it back to him. She'd told him then of how one night, when she'd been about six, she'd not been able to sleep. She'd come downstairs and found her father weeping silently over a picture of his late wife—Sam's mother.

Sam had said, 'He was talking to her...the picture...asking her what to do with me, asking her how he could cope because I was a girl. He said, *"If she was a boy I'd know what to do...but I don't know what to do or say to her."*'

Sam had sighed deeply. 'So I went upstairs to the bathroom that night, found a pair of scissors and cut all my hair off. It used to fall to my waist. When our housekeeper saw me in the morning she screamed and dropped a plate.'

Sam's mouth had twisted sadly. 'My father, though, he didn't even notice—too distracted with a problem he was trying to solve. I thought I could try to be a son for him...'

Rafaele could remember a falling sensation. Sam's inherent lack of self-confidence in her innate sensuality had all made sense. He too had known what it was like to have an absentee father. Even though he'd spent time with his father growing up, the man had been so embittered by his wife leaving him that he'd been no use to Rafaele and had rarely expressed much interest in his son. In some small part Rafaele knew that even resurrecting the family car industry had been a kind of effort to connect with his father.

It had been that weekend that Rafaele had let Sam stay in his *palazzo*. It had been that weekend that he'd postponed an important business trip because he'd wanted her too much to leave. And it was after that weekend, once he'd gained some distance from her, that he'd realised just how dangerous she was to him.

And he'd just proved that nothing had changed. She was still just as dangerous and he must never forget it.

The following day Milo was practically bursting with excitement at being in Rafaele's car. It was the latest model of the Falcone road car—the third to be rolled out since Rafaele had taken control of the bankrupt company.

It was completely impractical as far as children went, but Rafaele had surprised Sam. She'd seen that he'd got a child's car seat from somewhere and had it fitted into the backseat. Every time Sam looked around Milo just grinned at her like a loon. She shook her head ruefully as Rafaele negotiated out of the driveway and onto the main road with confident ease.

Sam tried to ignore his big hands on the wheel and gearstick. But there was something undeniably sexy about a man who handled a car well—and especially one like this, which was more like an art form than a car. Rafaele was a confident driver, and not the kind of person who felt the need for speed just to impress.

Happy sounds were coming from the back of the car—Milo imitating the engine. Sam felt a flutter near her heart and blocked it out. *Dangerous*. She still felt tense after that impassioned exchange the previous evening. Predictably, she hadn't been able to sleep well and she felt fuzzy now. She'd avoided looking directly at Rafaele this morning over breakfast, preferring to let Milo take centre stage, demanding the attention of this new, charismatic person in their midst.

Rafaele had seemed equally keen to be distracted, and Sam could only wonder if he'd taken anything of what she'd said to heart. Was he prepared to forgive her at all?

Sam noticed that Milo had gone silent behind them and looked back to see that he'd fallen asleep. Rafaele glanced her way and Sam quickly looked forward again, saying a little too breathlessly for her liking, 'He was so excited about today... He doesn't really nap any more but sometimes it catches up with him.'

She was babbling, and the thought of increased proximity to Rafaele when she started working with him to-

morrow made her feel panicky. She steeled herself and
turned to his proud profile. The profile of a great line of
aristocratic Italian ancestors.

'Look, Rafaele…about me working at the factory…'
She saw his jaw clench and rushed on. 'You said yourself
last night that you're only doing it to keep me where you
can see me. I can work perfectly well from the university.
After last night I can't see how our working together will
improve things.'

His hands clenched on the wheel now, and Sam looked
at them, so strong and large. She recalled how hot they'd
felt exploring her body.

Distracted, she almost missed it when Rafaele said in
a low voice, with clear reluctance, 'I shouldn't have said
that. It wasn't entirely true.'

Sam gulped and looked back at him. 'It wasn't?' Somewhere a tiny flame lit inside her, and against every atom
of self-preservation she couldn't douse it.

'After all,' he reminded her, 'I contacted you about
working for me before I knew about Milo and you refused to listen.'

The panic she'd felt then was still vivid. 'Yes,' she said
faintly. 'I…it was a shock to hear from you.'

Rafaele slanted her a look and said dryly, 'You don't
say.' He looked at the road again. 'But the fact remains
that I knew about your research. You were mentioned in
an article in *Automotive Monthly* and I realised that you
were leading the field in research into kinetic energy re-
covery systems.'

The little flame inside Sam sputtered. Of *course* he
hadn't been motivated by anything other than professional
interest. 'I see,' she responded. 'And that's why you wanted
to contact me?'

Rafaele shrugged minutely, his broad shoulders moving sinuously under his leather jacket, battered and worn

to an almost sensual texture. *Dammit*... Sam cursed herself. Why did everything have to return to all things physical even when he was wounding her with his words? She looked away resolutely.

He continued, 'I knew we were setting up in England, I figured you were still based here... It seemed like a logical choice to ask you to work for us again...'

Out of the corner of Sam's eye she saw Rafaele's hands tighten on the wheel again. His jaw clenched and then released.

'About last night—you were right. I agree that the past is past and we need to move on. I don't want Milo to pick up on the tension between us any more than you do.'

Something dangerous swooped inside Sam at hearing him acknowledge this. She recognised the mammoth effort he must be making to concede this.

'Thank you,' she said huskily. 'And I'll have to trust that you won't do anything to hurt Milo.'

The car was stopped at a red light now and Rafaele looked at her. 'Yes, you will. Hurting my son is the last thing in the world I want to do. It won't happen.'

The fierce light in his eyes awed Sam into silence. Eventually, she nodded, her throat feeling tight. 'Okay.'

A car horn tooted from behind them, and with unhurried nonchalance Rafaele released her from his gaze and moved on.

After a while Rafaele said in a low voice, 'And you *will* be coming to work with me, Sam...because I want you to.'

After a long moment Sam replied again. 'Okay.' In her wayward imagination she fancied that something had finally shifted between them, alleviating the ever-present tension.

They were silent for much of the rest of the journey, but something inside Sam had lessened slightly. And yet conversely she felt more vulnerable than ever.

She noticed that they were pulling into what looked like a stately home and raised a questioning brow at Rafaele, who answered, 'I asked my assistant to look up some things. It's an open house at weekends and they have a working farm. I thought Milo might like to see it.'

Milo had woken up a short while before, and from the backseat came an excited, 'Look, Mummy! Horsies!'

Sam saw Rafaele look to his son in the rearview mirror and the way his mouth curved into a smile. Her chest tightened and she explained, 'It's his other favourite thing in the world apart from cars. You're killing two birds with one stone.'

Rafaele looked at her for a long moment, his eyes lingering on her mouth until it tingled. Sam grew hot and flustered. Why was he teasing her with looks like this when he couldn't be less interested? Was it just something he turned on automatically when any woman with a pulse was nearby? It made her think of that angry kiss—how instantly she'd gone up in flames when he'd only been proving a point.

'Shouldn't you look where you're driving?' She sounded like a prim schoolmistress.

Rafaele eventually looked away, but not before purring with seductive arrogance, '*Cara*, I could drive blindfolded and not crash.'

This was what she remembered. Rafaele's easy and lethal brand of charm. Disgusted with herself, Sam faced forward and crossed her arms.

When he had parked and they'd got out, Milo clearly didn't know what to do first: stand and looking lovingly at the car, or go and see the animals. For a second he looked genuinely upset, overwhelmed with all these exciting choices. It made guilt lance Sam—fresh guilt—because the local park or swimming pool was about as exciting as it had got so far for Milo.

To Sam's surprise, before she could intervene, Rafaele bent down to Milo's level and said, '*Piccolino*, the car will still be here when we get back…so why don't we see the animals first, hmm?'

Milo's face cleared like a cloud passing over the sun and he smiled, showing his white baby teeth. 'Okey-dokey, horsies first.' And then he put his hand in Rafaele's and started pulling him the direction he wanted to go.

Sam caught the unguarded moment of emotion in Rafaele's eyes and her chest tightened at its significance. It was the first time Milo had reached out to touch him.

She followed them, doing up her slimline parka jacket and tried not to be affected by the image of the tall, powerful man, alongside the tiny, sturdy figure with identical dark hair.

Within a few hours Sam could see the beginnings of the hero-worship situation she'd predicted unfolding before her eyes. Milo had barely let go of Rafaele's hand and was now in his arms, pointing at the pigs in a mucky pen.

She was watching Rafaele for signs that this situation was getting old very quickly—she knew how demanding and energetic Milo could be—but she couldn't find any. Again she was stunned at his apparent easing into this whole situation.

Rafaele looked at her then and Sam coloured, more affected by seeing him with Milo in his arms than she cared to admit.

He looked grim and said, 'I think now is a good time.'

Instantly Sam understood. He wanted to tell Milo who he was. Panic flooded Sam. Until Milo knew Rafaele was his father it was as if she still had a way out—the possibility that this wasn't real. It was all a dream. But it wasn't, and she knew she couldn't fight him. He deserved for his son to know. And Milo deserved it too.

Jerkily, feeling clammy, Sam nodded her head. 'Okay.'

So when Milo had finished inspecting all the animals exhaustively they found a quiet spot to eat the food they'd got from the house's café and Sam explained gently to Milo that Rafaele was his father.

She could sense Rafaele's tension and her heart ached for him. Her conscience lambasted her again.

With all the unpredictability of a three-year-old though, Milo just blinked and looked from her to Rafaele before saying, 'Can we look at the horsies again?'

To his credit, Rafaele didn't look too surprised but when Milo had clambered off his chair to go and look at something she said, 'It's probably a lot for him to take in—'

But Rafaele cut her off, saying coolly, 'I know he took it in. I remember how much three-year-olds see and understand.'

He got up to follow Milo before Sam could make sense of his words and what he'd meant by them.

When they were back in the car Milo began chattering incessantly in the back.

'Rafelli, did you see the pigs? Rafelli, did you see the horsies and the goats? And the chickens?'

Sam looked out of the window, overcome with a surge of emotion. It was done. Rafaele truly was his father now. No going back. Tears pricked her eyes as the enormity of everything set in. She'd kept Milo from his own father for so long. Guilt was hot and acrid in her gut.

Suddenly her hand was taken in a much bigger, warmer one and her heart stopped.

'Sam?'

Panicked that he'd see her distress, Sam took her hand from his and rubbed at her eye, avoiding looking at him. Breezily she said, 'I'm fine. It's just some dust or something in my eye.'

CHAPTER SIX

Two weeks later Sam was trying to concentrate on test results and threw her pen down in disgust when her brain just refused to work. She got up from her desk in her decent-sized office at the factory and paced, rolling her head to ease out kinks as she did so.

It felt as if an age had passed since that day at the stately home. Within a few days Milo had been tentatively calling Rafaele *Daddy*, much to Bridie's beaming approval, Rafaele's delight and Sam's increasing sense of vulnerability.

Bridie had also paved the way for Sam to go to work with Rafaele every day, assuring her that she had nothing to worry about where Milo's care was concerned. So in the past two weeks a routine had developed where Rafaele took Milo to playschool, either with or without Sam, and then they left for work and returned in time for Milo's supper. Sam had put her foot down, though, and insisted that she still only do a half-day on Wednesdays as that had been her routine with Bridie.

And also she felt the need to establish some control when it felt as if Rafaele had comprehensively taken everything over. They'd even come home one evening to find a chef in the kitchen and Rafaele saying defensively something about it being unfair to expect Bridie to cook for them as well as taking care of Milo.

Needless to say Sam could see that Bridie was not far

behind Milo in the hero-worship stakes. Most evenings now Rafaele tucked Milo into bed and read him a story, making Sam feel redundant for the first time in a long time.

In the middle of all this change and turmoil was the sheer joy Sam felt at being back working on research within an environment where the actual cars and engines were only a short walk away. The scale of Rafaele's English factory had taken her breath away. It proved just how far he'd come even in three and a half years. Professionally she would have given her right arm to be part of this process, and now she was overseeing a group of mechanics and engineers, focusing their expertise on the most exciting developments in automotive technology, thanks to Rafaele's unlimited investment.

But overshadowing everything was the fact that she was working for Rafaele. Back in a place where she'd never expected or wanted to be. She felt as if she was that girl all over again—that naive student, obsessed with her boss. Watching out for him. Aware of him. Blushing when their gazes met. It was galling and humiliating. Especially when Rafaele appeared so cool and seemed to be making every effort to steer well clear of Sam. Only addressing her in groups of people. Never seeking her out alone.

Even on their car rides to the factory and back their conversation centred mainly around Milo or work.

Her hands clenched to fists now, even as her whole body seemed to ache. She was glad. She *was.* She didn't want history to repeat itself. Not in a million years. It had almost been easier when Rafaele had hated her; now that they were in this uneasy truce it was so much more confusing to deal with.

Sam noticed the clock on the wall then, and saw how late it was. Normally Rafaele's assistant would have rung to inform her that he was leaving by now. Giving up any pretence that she could continue to work while waiting,

Sam decided to pack up and find him herself. She would inform him she was going home. He'd offered her one of the cars if she wished, so now perhaps it was time to assert some more independence from him.

Heading for his office, she saw it was quiet all around, most of the other staff and the main engineers and mechanics having left. His own secretary's desk was clear and empty in the plush anteroom of his office.

She hesitated for a second outside his door and then knocked. After a few seconds she heard him call abruptly, 'Come in.'

Rafaele glanced up from his phone call, frowning slightly at the interruption, and then when Sam walked in his whole body reacted, making a complete mockery of any illusion of control over his rogue hormones. She stopped in her tracks and made a motion to leave again, seeing he was on the phone, but everything within him rejected that and he held up his finger, indicating for her to wait.

She closed the door behind her and he couldn't stop the anticipation spiking in his blood. For two weeks now Rafaele had thought he was doing a good job of avoiding her. But it didn't matter how much space he put between them; he saw her everywhere. Worst of all was in the house at night—that cosy, domestic house, with his son sleeping just down the hall—when all he could think about doing was going into Sam's room, stripping her bare and sinking deep between her long legs.

His body was hardening even now, shaming him with his lack of control. The person on the other end of the phone continued talking but they might as well have been talking the language of the Dodo for all Rafaele heard. His gaze travelled down Sam's back and legs hungrily, taking in her slim build and the sweet lush curve of her buttocks as she turned away to look at a model of one of the first cars he'd designed.

When she turned back slightly he could see the profile swell of her breasts and immediately a memory came back, of spilling drops of Prosecco onto one pebbled nipple, making it grow hard— Sweat broke out on Rafaele's upper lip. This was untenable.

Abruptly he terminated the phone conversation, giving up any pretence of control. Sam had turned around to face him and he asked, more curtly than he'd intended, 'What do you want?'

Her face flushed and Rafaele pushed down the lurch of his conscience. Damn her and the way she did that, making him feel like a heel.

'I just…it's after six. We usually leave before now.'

The *we* struck him somewhere forcibly. He stood up and saw how Sam's eyes widened. His body reacted to that look and he cursed her again.

He reacted viscerally. 'I think this is a mistake.'

She frowned. 'What's a mistake?'

'You…here.' Dammit, he couldn't even string a coherent sentence together. The longer she stood there, the more he was imagining her naked, opening up to him, giving him the release he'd only ever found with her. Seeing her here at the factory these past two weeks had been giving him moments of severe *déjà vu*.

She was still frowning, but had gone still. 'Me…here… What exactly do you mean, Rafaele?'

Why was it that the way she said his name in that soft, low voice seemed to curl around his senses, making everything even more heightened?

He gritted out, through the waves of need assailing him, 'I shouldn't have insisted you work here. It was a bad idea.'

The unmistakable flare of hurt made her eyes glow

bright grey for a moment, reminding Rafaele uncomfortably of another day, in another office, four years before.

Stiffly she said, 'I thought I was doing everything you wanted—we set up the research facility here in one week. I know it still needs more work, but it's only been two weeks—'

Rafaele slashed a hand, making her stop. 'It's not that.'

Sounding wounded, she said, 'Well, what, then?'

Rafaele wanted to laugh. Could she not see how ravenous he was for her? He felt like a beast, panting for its prey.

He smiled grimly. 'It's you. Uniquely. I thought I could do this. But I can't. I think you should go back to the university…someone else can take over here.'

Sam straightened before him and her eyes flashed—but with anger and something more indefinable this time.

'You insisted on turning my world upside down, Rafaele, and now, just because you can't abide the sight of me, you think you can cast me out again? It seems as if you rather overestimated your desire for control, doesn't it? Well, if you've quite decided where it is you want me then don't worry. I'll be only too happy to get out of your way.'

Sam was quivering with impotent rage. She wanted to go over and slap Rafaele. Hard. It could be four years ago all over again. With nothing learned in the meantime. She was standing before Rafaele in his office and he was basically rejecting her. Again.

And, like before, Sam was terrified she'd crumple before him, so she fled for the door. But when she tried to open it with clammy hands it slammed shut again, and she squealed with shock when she felt a solid, hard presence behind her.

She whirled around to find her eye level at Rafaele's broad chest and looked up. Emotion was high in her throat. Her eyes were burning. 'Let me out of here, *now*.'

The hurt that had gripped her like a vice in her belly at hearing him say so starkly that he basically couldn't stand to see her every day was still like acid.

'You've got it wrong,' he gritted out, jaw tight, seemingly oblivious to what she'd just said. His hand was snaking around her neck under her hair, making her breath catch. His eyes were like green gems. Glittering.

Sam swallowed the pain, determined he wouldn't see it, but she was acutely aware of how close he was—almost close enough for his chest to touch her breasts. They tightened, growing heavy, the nipples pebbling into hard points.

'Got what wrong?' she spat out.

'I didn't overestimate my desire for control... I overestimated my ability to resist you.'

Sam blinked. But now Rafaele's chest was touching her breasts and she couldn't think straight. His hand tightened on her neck and his face was coming closer. Her lips tingled in anticipation. All the blood in her body was pooling between her legs, making her hot and ready.

Fighting the intense desire not to question this, Sam put her hands on Rafaele's chest. 'Wait...' she got out painfully. 'What are you doing?'

Rafaele's breath feathered over her mouth, making her fingers want to curl into his chest. She couldn't seem to take her eyes away from his, green boring into grey, making reality melt away.

Sam struggled to make sense of this, when only moments ago she'd believed he wanted her out of his sight because something about her repulsed him. 'But you don't... you don't really want me.'

He asked, almost bitterly, 'Don't I?'

Confusion filled Sam—and a very treacherous flame of hope. She fought it desperately, fearing exposure. She pushed against him but he was like steel. 'Let me *go*, Rafaele. I won't be your substitute lover just because you're turned on for five seconds. I don't like to repeat mistakes.'

Rafaele laughed again and it was unbearably harsh, scraping over Sam's sensitised skin like sandpaper.

'Five seconds? Try four years, Sam—four years of an ache that never went away, no matter how much I tried to deny it...no matter how many times I tried to eclipse it...'

His voice had become guttural, thick. Sam couldn't fully process his words, but somewhere deep inside her they did resonate, and she felt something break apart— some resistance she'd been clinging onto.

'I want you, Sam, and I know you want me too.'

And then his mouth was on hers and it was desperate, forceful. Like before, but *not*. Without the intense anger and recrimination behind it. And once again, like a lemming jumping over a cliff to certain death, Sam couldn't help but respond. And she couldn't deny the fierce burst of primal pleasure within her, deep inside where she'd locked it away.

But the kiss didn't stay forceful. Rafaele drew back, breathing harshly, and Sam followed him, too much on fire to be embarrassed by how much she wanted him. He wanted her, and the knowledge sang in her blood. She had nothing to be ashamed of.

Rafaele bent close again, and when he pressed a hot kiss to her neck Sam felt his hand do something behind her. She heard the snick of the lock in the door. It should have made alarm bells ring in her head. It should have reminded her of similar heated moments in the past. But it didn't. Or she wouldn't let it. She was weak and she'd ached for this for too long. Long nights when Milo hadn't wanted to sleep and she'd walked up and down, breasts sore from breast-feeding, but aching, too, for another far more adult touch.

Rafaele straightened and with an enigmatic look took Sam by the hand. For a second she felt absurdly shy and bit her lip. Rafaele stopped and reached out, freeing her lip with his thumb.

He muttered, '*Dio*, I've missed that.' And Sam's insides combusted.

He drew her over towards the desk and then turned to take Sam's bag off her shoulder, along with her jacket. They fell to the floor. Sam felt the back of the desk against her buttocks. Her legs were wobbly.

Rafaele cupped her face and jaw with his hands and then his mouth was on hers again, hot and hard, firm but soft. Demanding and getting a response that she had no control over. Her tongue stroked along his. She was desperate to taste every inch of him, revelling in the spiralling heat inside her. She was vaguely aware of her questing hands going to his chest, exulting in the feel of rock-hard muscle, her fingers finding buttons and opening them so that she could reach in and explore, feel that hair-roughened skin.

Rafaele's hands moved down, coming to her buttocks, kneading them, and then lifting her so that she rested on the desk. He came closer, wedging himself between her legs so that his belt buckle was hard against her belly. Below, the most potent part of his anatomy was also hard, right there between her legs, constrained by their clothes and making her want to strip everything between them away.

One of his hands clasped her head, tilting it so that he had deeper access. His tongue was mimicking another part of his anatomy now, and his hips were moving against her, making her squirm and whimper softly as the fever of desire rose within her.

Suddenly Rafaele pulled away and Sam looked up through a heat haze, aware of her heart pounding and her ragged breath. Rafaele's shirt hung half open.

'I need to see you,' he said thickly, and began to undo the buttons on her shirt.

As the backs of his hands brushed against her breasts she shivered minutely at the exquisite sensation, already imagining him touching them with his hands...his mouth and tongue.

Her shirt was drawn off and her bra dispensed with in an economy of movement, and then he just looked at her for a long moment, with an enigmatic expression that made butterflies erupt in Sam's belly. About to scream with the mounting tension, she felt Rafaele's hand finally cup her breast and shards of sensation rushed through her body. She tensed and arched her back, subconsciously begging him...and he needed no encouragement.

Cupping the full mound of firm flesh, Rafaele bent his head and surrounded that tight peak in moist heat. The feel of his intense hot sucking made Sam cry out.

Blindly, while Rafaele's mouth was on her breast, Sam reached for his belt and undid it, her hands and fingers clumsy. She pulled it free of his trousers and it dropped to the floor, but before she could put her hands to his fly he was standing up again and helping her, pushing his trousers down, leaving him bared to her hungry gaze. *Dear Lord*. He was as magnificent as she remembered. Thick and long and hard. For *her*.

Sam felt hot, as if she was on fire. She moved her numb fingers to Rafaele's shirt buttons, wanting to finish undressing him. Her breath was loud in the quiet of the office. All that mattered to Sam was getting Rafaele bared to her, and when she finally pushed his shirt open and off his shoulders she breathed in deeply, her hands smoothing over hard musculature roughened with dark hair, nipples erect and hard.

Unable to resist the lure, Sam explored with her tongue around those hard pieces of puckered flesh, aware of Rafaele's hand on her head. He sucked in a breath, making his broad chest swell. He was so sensitive there. Sam moved her mouth up now, stretching her whole body, trailing kisses and tasting with her tongue along his throat, discovering the hard resoluteness of his stubbled jaw grazing her delicate skin.

Her hands on his head drew him down. She was searching for his mouth again, like a blind person looking for water in a desert. Sucking him deep into her own mouth, Sam could feel his erection strain against her, and she dropped one hand to put it around him, feeling him jerk with tension.

'Sam…'

She almost didn't recognise his voice. It sounded so tortured. Sam tore her mouth away from his to look up and she was dizzy with need and lust. It was just them and this insane desire. He was so firm in her hand, so strong, and her mouth watered when she remembered how she'd tasted him before, how she'd sucked that head into her mouth, her tongue swirling and exploring around the tip, her hand pumping him the way he'd shown her…

She didn't even realise her hand was moving rythmically until he tipped up her chin with his fingers and said, 'I need to be inside you.'

Sam's sex throbbed. 'Yes,' she breathed, lifting her hips to help Rafaele when he went to pull her trousers and panties off. She was vaguely surprised she still had them on, that they hadn't melted off her before now.

Rafaele took himself in his hand—an unashamed and utterly masculine gesture. Sam was sitting on the desk naked, legs spread like a wanton, but she couldn't drum up any concern. She wanted him inside her so badly. Rafaele ran his hand down over her quivering body, teasing her until she bit her lip. He pushed her legs apart further and looked at her.

He stroked one hand up her inner thigh and let it rest for a moment at the tantalising juncture before his long fingers explored the wetness at her core—and then in one move he thrust them inside her.

Sam gasped and grabbed onto Rafaele's shoulders, unable to look away from that glittering, possessive green gaze. His fingers moved in and out, and her body started to clench around them, the anticipation building to fever-pitch.

On some level Sam rejected this. She didn't want to splinter apart while Rafaele looked on. She took his hand away from her and said roughly, 'No—not like this. I'll come when you come.'

Rafaele smiled and it was fierce. The smile of a warrior. He took her mouth in another devastating kiss and her wetness was on the fingers that he wrapped tight around her hips. Rafaele thrust deep inside her in one cataclysmic move and swallowed her scream of pleasure, his hand holding her steady when she went so taut with excitement that she thought she'd splinter apart there and then, despite her brave words.

But slowly, inexorably, expertly, Rafaele drew her back from that brink and then, with slow, measured, devastating thrusts of his body into hers he rewound that tension inside her until it built up higher and higher all over again.

Sam wrapped her legs around Rafaele's waist, her ankles crossed, her feet digging into his hard backside, urging him on, begging without words for him to go deeper, harder. Pushing her away from him slightly, but supporting her with an arm around her, he thrust harder and deeper.

Sam's head went back. Her eyes closed. She couldn't take it—couldn't articulate what she needed. She needed to come so badly, but Rafaele was relentless. She knew she was only seconds from begging. Overwhelmed, she felt tears prick her eyes—and then Rafaele thrust so deep it felt as if he touched her heart.

Eyes flying open, tendons going taut all over her body,

Sam came in a dizzying, blinding crescendo of pleasure so intense she couldn't breathe. She gasped and felt Rafaele thrust deep again, sending her spiralling into an even higher dimension of pleasure. His body jerked between her legs and she felt her endless pulsating orgasm milking him of his essence, which was a warm flood inside her.

In the aftermath of that shattering crescendo Sam barely knew which way was up. Her legs were still locked around his slim hips. Rafaele's head was buried in her neck and she had the strongest urge to reach out and touch his hair, but when she lifted a hand it was trembling too much.

His chest was heaving and damp against hers. Her breasts were tender. Rafaele was still hard inside her, his strength ebbing slowly. And then suddenly he reared back, eyes wild, making Sam wince as he broke the connection between their bodies.

'Protection. We didn't use protection.'

Sam looked at him and went icy, before reason and sanity broke through. Relief was tinged with something bittersweet. 'No,' she breathed, 'It's okay, I'm…safe.'

She bit her lip, suddenly acutely aware of how she was balancing precariously on the desk with Rafaele's eyes on her. She felt raw, as if a layer of skin had been stripped off her body. She clenched her hands.

'Are you sure?' he demanded.

Sam forced herself to look at Rafaele. Her mouth twisted. 'Yes. I'm sure. My period just finished.'

He sighed deeply. 'Okay.'

Sam couldn't keep the bitterness out of her voice. 'You believe me, then?'

He paused in reaching down to grab some clothes and looked at her. 'I believe you. I don't think you'd want to repeat history any more than I would.'

The words shouldn't have hurt her. Much as his earlier

words shouldn't have hurt her. But they did. Sam didn't want to question why.

Grimacing slightly when her muscles protested, she stood shakily from the desk and took her shirt and bra from Rafaele's outstretched hand.

She couldn't look at him. Face burning, she turned away to put on her clothes and castigated herself. She was repeating history right here, right now. Making love with him in his office exactly like she used to. She could remember what it had been like to go back onto the factory floor, feeling exhilarated and shamed all at once, as if a brand on her forehead marked her as some sort of fallen woman. The boss's concubine.

She pulled on her pants and trousers with clumsy fingers, aware of Rafaele just feet away, dressing himself, sheathing that amazing body again.

When she was dressed he said coolly from behind her, 'Shall we go?'

Sam steeled herself and turned around to see Rafaele looking hardly rumpled, his hair only slightly messy. She knew she must look as if she'd just been pulled through a hedge backwards. The tang of sex was in the air and it should have sickened her, but it didn't. It made her crave more.

'Yes,' she said quickly, before he could see how vulnerable she felt.

Rafaele burned with recrimination as he negotiated his car out of the factory in the dark with Sam beside him, tight-lipped. His recrimination was not for what had happened; he'd do that again right now if he could. His recrimination was for the way it had happened. He'd behaved like a teenage boy, drooling over his first lay with finesse the last thing on his mind.

When she'd asked him just now if he believed her, his

reaction had been knee-jerk and not fair. He was already repeating history with bells on, and he knew he wouldn't have the strength to resist her even if he wanted to.

It had been a miracle that he'd had the control to make sure Sam had come first—but then he recalled how ready to explode she'd been when he'd just touched her with his fingers. Just like that he was rewarded with a fresh, raging erection and had to shift to cover it in the gloom of the interior of the car.

He'd taken Sam *on his desk*. He'd only ever let one other woman get to him at work—the same woman. Until he'd met Sam his life had been strictly compartmentalised into work and pleasure. That pleasure had been fleeting and completely within his control. As soon as he'd laid eyes on her, though, the lines had blurred into one.

He could still remember the cold, clammy panic that last weekend four years ago at finding himself waking in his own bed with Sam wrapped around him like a vine. Far from precipitating repugnance, he'd felt curiously at peace. Until he'd realised the significance of that and that peace had been shattered. He'd postponed an important meeting that weekend to spend it with Sam. He'd even turned off his phone. Had not checked e-mails. He'd gone incommunicado. For the first time. For a woman.

It had been that which had made something go cold in his chest. Realising how far off his own strict path he'd gone.

Even now he was aware of that, but also aware of Sam's slim supple thighs in her black trousers next to him. Albeit slanted away, as if she was avoiding coming any closer than she had to in the small, intimate space.

Dio. If she was his he'd make her wear skirts and dresses all the time, so that all he'd have to do would be to slide his hand— *If she was his*. Rafaele let the car swerve momentarily and very uncharacteristically as that thought slid home with all the devastation of a stealth bomb.

He could feel Sam's quick glance of concern and imagine her frowning.

'Sorry,' he muttered, and regained control of himself. He could see from the corner of his eye that Sam had crossed her arms over her breasts. She was so tense he fancied she might crack in two if he touched her.

Her silence was getting to him, making his nerves wind tight inside him. He wanted to provoke her—get her to acknowledge what had just happened. What it possibly meant to her. Was the same round of unwelcome memories dominating *her* head?

Injecting his voice with an insouciance he didn't feel, Rafaele asked, 'Don't tell me you're already regretting what happened, *cara*.'

She snapped at him, 'Is it that obvious?'

Rafaele's mouth tightened in rejection of that, despite his recent thoughts. 'It was inevitable and you know it. It's been building between us from the moment we saw each other again.'

He glanced at Sam and their eyes met. A jolt of electricity shot straight to Rafaele's groin.

She hissed at him, 'It was *not* inevitable. It was a momentary piece of very bad judgment. You were obviously feeling frustrated—maybe it's because you've been forced to move to the suburbs so you can't entertain your mistress.'

Rage was building inside Rafaele and he responded with a snarl, 'I don't have a mistress at the moment.'

Sam sniffed. 'Maybe not, but I'm sure there's been a number in the last four years.'

And not one of them Rafaele could remember right now. But if he was a painter he could paint Sam's naked body with his eyes closed. He recalled seeing Sam bite her lip and how he'd let slip *'I've missed this.'* He'd also told her that no one had come close to her in four years. Then he'd all but admitted that he'd used other women to try and forget her. His belly curdled.

He ground out, 'Are you expecting me to believe that you've been celibate for four years?' He glanced at her and saw her go pale in the gloom. 'Well? Have you?'

Sam stared straight ahead. Stonily. 'Of course not. There was someone…a while ago.'

For a second Rafaele only heard a roaring in his ears. He saw red. He almost gave in to the impulse to swerve the car to the kerb. He'd fully expected her to say *of course not*, and his own hypocrisy mocked him. But, he told himself savagely, *he* hadn't given birth to a baby.

He was aware that irrational emotions were clouding his normally perfectly liberal views and it was not something Rafaele welcomed.

'Who was he?' he bit out, knuckles white under the skin of his fingers on the wheel. Just the thought of Sam even kissing someone else was making him incandescent.

'He was a colleague. He's a single parent too…we bonded over that.'

Rafaele felt as if a red-hot poker had been stabbed into his belly. In a calm voice, belying the strength of his emotions, Rafaele said, 'You were a single parent by choice, Samantha. You are *not* a single parent any more.'

Rafaele struggled to control himself. He wanted to demand Sam tell him more—how many times? Where? When?

As if sensing his intense interest, Sam blurted out, 'It didn't amount to anything. It was just one time. We went to a hotel for an afternoon and to be perfectly honest it was horrible. It felt…sordid.'

She clamped her mouth shut again and Rafaele realised he was holding his breath. He let it out in one long shud-

dery breath. His hands relaxed. Even though he still wanted
to find this faceless, nameless person and throw him up
against a wall.

From the moment Sam had stepped into his office earlier he'd been on fire. The culmination of weeks of build-
up. The inferno inside him had been too strong to ignore.
Feeling Sam in his arms, her mouth under his, opening up
to him, pressing herself against him… He'd been thrusting into the tight, slick heat that he'd never forgotten right
there on his desk before he'd even really acknowledged
what was happening. He'd been in the grip of something
more powerful than his rational mind.

They hadn't even used protection. Sam was the only
woman that had ever happened with, and the result of that
was probably being put to bed right now. He looked at Sam
again and saw that she was still pale, a pulse throbbing
at the base of her neck. She'd uncrossed her arms finally
and her breasts rose and fell a little too quickly, giving
her away. They were stopped in traffic and he reached
over and took her hand, gripping it when she would have
pulled away.

He forced her to look at him and her eyes were huge.
Rafaele saw something unguarded in their depths for a
split second, but then it was gone and he crushed down
the feeling of something resonating deep inside him. The
jealousy he felt still burned in his gut.

He wanted to hate Sam for ever appearing in his life
to disrupt his ordered and well-run world. A world where
nothing had mattered except rebuilding Falcone Industries
and ensuring that he would never be ruined like his father.
Sam had jeopardised that for a brief moment in time and
now it was happening all over again. But he found that he
couldn't hate her for that any more because Milo existed.
And because he wanted her.

'Let me go, Rafaele,' Sam breathed.

Never resounded in his head before he could stop it. He kept his gaze on hers, slightly discomfited that it wasn't harder to do so. Usually he avoided women's probing looks. But not this one. Something solidified within him. He couldn't *not* have Sam again after that passionate interlude. It was an impossible prospect.

'No, Sam.'

He lifted her resisting hand and brought it to his mouth, pressed his lips to her palm. Her scent made him harder. His tongue flicked out and he tasted her skin, fancying he could distinguish her musky heat—or was that just her arousal he could smell?

Frustration at the prospect of the weekend ahead gripped him. He couldn't make love to her in the house. Not while his son lay sleeping. The thought of Milo waking and witnessing how feral Rafaele felt around Sam was anathema after his own experience of being that small and witnessing his father's breakdown.

Sam's eyes grew wide. Glittering. Pupils dilating. They were distracting him. Making him regret that he couldn't make love with her again for at least a few days. It would not happen in his office again. Never again. But they weren't done—not by a long shot.

'I'm not letting you go. Not until this is well and truly burnt out between us. I let you go too soon once before and I won't make that mistake again.'

The lights went green and Rafaele let Sam's hand go. He turned his attention to the road again and the car moved smoothly forward.

Sam clasped her tingling hand and turned her head, staring straight in front of her. Her whole body was still deeply sensitised after what had happened and yet she already felt ravenous for more. His words sank in: *I let you go too soon.*

He'd said something earlier about trying to eclipse her memory... His admission made her heart race pathetically.

And why on earth had she spilled her guts about her one very sad attempt at another relationship? To score points? To try and convince Rafaele that he hadn't dominated her life so totally?

But that was what she *had* attempted to do with the perfectly nice and normal Max. He'd caught her at a particularly vulnerable moment one day. Sam had seen a random newspaper report documenting the launch of a new Falcone car and there had been a picture of Rafaele with his arm around some gorgeous blonde model.

More than upset, and disturbed that she was still affected by him and the memories which would not abate after so much time, Sam had recklessly taken Max up on his offer of dinner. After a few weeks of pleasant but not earth-shattering dating Sam had felt a need to try and prove to herself that her memory of Rafaele was a mirage. That surely any other man could match him in bed and then she would not feel such a sense of loss, that she'd never experience such heights again.

It had been her suggestion to meet in a hotel one afternoon. As if they were both married and having an affair. But she'd thought it practical, considering their children were in their own homes, being minded. And Sam hadn't felt at all comfortable with introducing Max to Milo...even though he'd been hinting that the time to do so had come.

The afternoon had been awkward and horrendous from the first moment. Completely underwhelming. Disgusted with herself, because she had known that she'd acted out of weakness, Sam had called it off there and then.

Something very dangerous and fragile fluttered in the vicinity of her heart, where she'd blocked off any emotions for Rafaele a long time ago. Sam had fancied for a second that he had appeared jealous when she'd men-

tioned Max…which was ridiculous. What right had he to
be jealous? He'd given up that right when he'd been with
a woman less than a week after letting her go.

Sam took a deep breath and tried to crush the nebu-
lous and very dangerous feeling growing within her. She
would be the biggest fool on this planet if she was to read
anything into Rafaele's possessive gesture and demeanour
just now. As he'd said himself, he was only interested in
whatever this was between them until it burnt out.

As Sam knew to her cost it was far more likely to burn
out for him than for her, and she'd be left picking up the
pieces again—except this time it would be so much worse
because they were forever bound together now through
Milo, and she had a very sick feeling that she was in danger of falling for him all over again. Or, more accurately,
that she'd never stopped.

She went cold inside to think that perhaps part of her
reluctance to tell him about Milo had been to avoid this
very selfish scenario.

Rafaele smoothly drove the car into the space outside
her front door and Sam blinked. She hadn't even been
aware of the journey. Just then a curtain moved and Sam
saw Milo's small face appear, wearing a huge grin. Her
heart clenched hard. She could imagine him declaring excitedly, *'Daddy's home!'* as he'd been doing for the past
few days according to an approving Bridie, who seemed to
see nothing but good in Rafaele's appearance in their lives.

It was Friday. They had a weekend to get through now,
and Sam had no expectation that Rafaele would be sneak-
ing in through her bedroom door at night to pick up where
they'd left off. She knew from experience that he liked to
keep her a secret, on the periphery of his world.

Sam took a deep breath and schooled her features, hoping that Rafaele would never guess the extent of her turbulence around him, or that even now she ached between

her legs for one of his hands to press against her and alleviate her mounting frustration.

The fact that she was back in a place she'd clawed her way out of four years before was not a welcome revelation. At all.

CHAPTER SEVEN

On Sunday Sam was folding laundry in the little utility room off the kitchen. Rafaele had taken Milo swimming on his own earlier, and since they'd come home they'd played with Milo's cars in the sitting room. Now he was putting him to bed.

She'd felt like a cat on a hot tin roof all weekend. Lying in bed at night, *aching* with frustration. Locking her muscles to avoid walking down the hall to Rafaele's room to beg him to make love to her. She refused to give herself away so spectacularly. And she'd been right. He'd treated her coolly all weekend, clearly reluctant to draw what had happened in his office into the domestic sphere.

Sam was only good enough within an environment which suited him. Nothing had changed. The bitterness that scored her shocked her with its intensity. Her emotions were see-sawing all over the place.

What *hadn't* helped was the little surprise Rafaele had lined up when they'd woken that morning. The sleek supercar Rafaele had been using since he'd appeared in their lives had been replaced, probably by some hardworking minion, with a far more sedate *family* car.

'What's this?' Sam had asked faintly from the front door as Rafaele had deftly strapped Milo into his car seat to take him swimming.

He'd cast her a quick dry glance. 'It's a car, Sam. A more practical car, I think you'll agree, for a child…'

Sam had felt as if she'd just tipped over the edge of a precipice. All she'd been able to think about after they'd left, with an ecstatic Milo in the back, was of how Rafaele—one of the most Alpha male men she'd ever met, if not *the* most—had segued from playboy with a fast car into man with a child and a safety-conscious car without turning a hair. And somehow that had made Sam more nervous than anything else. She was too scared to look at all the implications and what they might mean…

She heard a noise then and tensed as she sensed Rafaele's presence behind her in the kitchen. She felt far too vulnerable to face him right now.

'I want you and Milo to come to Milan with me.'

Sam went very still for a moment, and then proceeded to fold a sheet as if he *hadn't* just dropped a bomb from a great height. Irritation with herself, with him, at the sexual frustration clawing at her insides, laced her voice. 'What are you talking about, Rafaele? We can't just go to Milan with you.'

Sounding impatient, Rafaele said, 'Sam, I can't talk to your back.' His voice changed and grew rougher. 'As delectable as it is. And your bottom in those jeans… *Dio*, do you know how hard it's been not to touch you all weekend?'

That made Sam whirl around, her blood heating instantaneously and rushing to every erogenous zone she had. She dropped the sheet from nerveless hands.

Despite her own craving need all weekend she hissed, 'Stop it. You can't talk to me like that. Not here, with Milo in the house.'

Rafaele was leaning against the doorjamb, far too close. His eyes narrowed on her, taking in her jeans and shirt. Grimly he admitted, 'I know. That's precisely why I restrained myself.'

Something gave way inside Sam at hearing him admit that his concern for Milo had been uppermost. It made her feel exposed, vulnerable. Between her legs she throbbed almost painfully.

Sam picked up the sheet and thrust it at Rafaele's chest. 'Here's some fresh linen for your bed.'

Rafaele caught the linen when it would have dropped to the ground again. His mouth had gone flat and tight.

'Well? Did you hear what I said about Milan? I want you and Milo to come with me this week.'

The thought of going back to the scene of the crime made Sam's emotions seesaw even more. She turned around again and blurted out, 'It's not practical, Rafaele. You can't just announce—'

'*Dio*, Sam.'

Sam let out a small squeak of surprise at Rafaele's guttural voice and saw the linen she'd just shoved at him sail over her head to land back on the pile haphazardly. Then she felt big hands swing her round until she was looking up in his grim face.

'Sam, I—' He stopped. His eyes went to her mouth and then he just said, *'Dio!'* again, before muttering something else in Italian and then pulling her into him.

His mouth was on hers, branding her, and she was up in flames in an instant, every point of her body straining to be closer to his hard form.

With a moan of helpless need and self-derision Sam submitted to the practised and expert ministrations of Rafaele's wicked mouth and tongue. Some tiny morsel of self-preservation eventually impinged on the heat and gave Sam the strength to pull free. She looked up into Rafaele's face and almost melted there and then at the sight of the feral look in his eyes. She put a hand to his chest, but that was worse when she felt his heart pounding.

'We can't. Not here...'

Rafaele smiled, but it was humourless. 'Maybe we'll have to book a hotel as you're partial to that kind of thing.'

That gave Sam the impetus to move, and she scooted out of the small space and rounded on Rafaele, arms crossed over the betraying throb of her breasts. Her voice was low with anger. 'You have no right to judge me when you were jumping into bed with someone new barely a week after I left Italy.'

Rafaele frowned. He looked volcanic. 'What the hell are you talking about? I wasn't with anyone.'

Sam emitted a curt laugh and tried to hide the flare of something pathetic within her. *Hope.* 'Well, that's not what it looked like—you were photographed all over the place with some Italian TV personality.'

Rafaele opened his mouth to speak but Sam put up a hand, stopping him.

Fiercely, she said, 'I don't care, Rafaele.' *Liar.*

Irrational guilt over her own liaison made her even angrier.

'Even if I had told you about Milo, it wasn't as if we were going to become some happy family. You told me what you thought of marriage and how you never wanted it in your life.'

Sam stopped, breathing heavily, and saw how Rafaele's face had become shuttered. Clearly he didn't like to be reminded of that.

'I seem to recall you agreeing fervently, Sam. Something about how seeing your father weep over your mother's picture had made you dread ever investing so much in one person only to lose them and be lonely for the rest of your life?'

Sam's insides contracted. She felt dizzy for a second and then mortification rushed through her like a shameful tide. She'd been so *open* with him. Had told him every little thing. As if he'd even been interested! Wasn't that exactly what she'd done, though? After a mere month in this man's bed she'd been ready to invest everything in him, only to realise how far off-base she'd been.

Panicking, she said the first thing she could think of to try and get them off this topic. 'What did you mean... about Milan?'

Rafaele's jaw clenched, but to her intense relief he appeared prepared to let it go.

'I want to take Milo to meet his grandfather—my father. It's going to come out sooner or later in the press that I have a son and I'd like Umberto to meet him before that happens. Also, he is old and frail...I'm conscious of his mortality.'

The words were delivered dispassionately enough to shock Sam slightly. Rafaele had never spoken of his father much before, except to say that he lived in a place called Bergamo, not far from Milan, and that he'd moved away after the family business had disintegrated and they'd lost everything. Sam knew that one of the first things Rafaele had done was to buy back the Falcone *palazzo* just outside Milan, as that was where he'd lived four years ago.

She hadn't met Umberto Falcone during the time she'd been with Rafaele, and against her better judgment her interest was piqued at the thought of seeing this tantalising glimpse of another aspect of Rafaele's life. And also to acknowledge that Milo had one grandparent still alive.

Rafaele continued, 'He's coming to Milan next week for a routine medical check-up and he's staying at the family *palazzo* just outside the city. I have to go back for a few days to attend a board meeting and drop in on the factory there. It would be a perfect opportunity to do this.'

She still resisted, despite being intrigued. 'Perfect for you, maybe... Milo has playschool, a routine. And what about my work?'

Rafaele's lip curled. 'Please—do you really expect me

to believe that Milo will be irreparably damaged by missing a few days of playschool? And...' those laser-like eyes narrowed on her '...I think that your boss would be very amenable to you taking the time off.'

Looking smug, Rafaele delivered the final nail in the coffin of Sam's hopes to escape.

'I spoke with Bridie about it when we met her outside just a while ago and she said she'd be only too happy to come to Italy with us and help watch Milo. She confided that as a devout Catholic she's always wanted to visit Rome, and I promised her we could make a stop there on the way back...'

Sam clenched her hands into fists at her sides. 'That's low-down and dirty manipulation, Rafaele.'

He shrugged lightly. 'Call it what you want, Sam, but I believe I'm entitled to a little "manipulation". You, Milo and Bridie are coming to Italy with me in two days' time so you'd better get prepared.'

Sam watched Rafaele turn and walk out and welcomed the rush of anger. No doubt he'd been planning this all along, lulling her into a false sense of security by moving into the house, demonstrating his capacity to compromise for his son's sake. Rafaele was just showing his true colours now: his desire to dominate.

But worse, much worse than that, was the prospect of how hard it would be to return to the place where it had all started. If she was barely holding it together here, how would she manage when she was face to face with the past?

Two days later, in accordance with Rafaele's autocratic decree, they were on a private plane belonging to Rafaele's younger half-brother, the Greek aviation and travel billionaire Alexio Christakos.

Bridie was in silent raptures over the plush luxuriousness of it all and Milo was like a bottle of shaken-up lemonade—about to fizz over at any moment. Every day for him at the moment seemed to bring nothing but untold treasures, and Sam looked at him kneeling on the seat beside her now, watching the world get smaller and smaller beneath them.

It was his first time on a plane and Milo automatically looked for his new favourite person on the planet: Rafaele. Pointing with a chubby finger, he said, 'Look, Daddy, *look!*'

Sam's heart squeezed so tight she had to put a hand there, as if that could assuage the bittersweet pain and the anxiety. How could she trust that Rafaele wouldn't grow bored and disappear from their lives, leaving Milo bereft? *And her...* Sam didn't even want to go there.

They were cruising now, and Rafaele stood up and managed to dwarf the very comfortable ten-seater plane. He held out a hand to Milo. 'Do you want to see the cockpit?'

He'd barely stopped talking before Milo had leapt off the seat and run to him. Rafaele picked him up. Milo didn't even look to Sam for reassurance.

Sam felt silly tears prick her eyes and turned away, but she heard Bridie saying quietly from across the small aisle, 'He's a good man. He'll take care of you both.'

Sam fought valiantly for control and looked at Bridie, gave her a watery smile. She couldn't hide anything from this woman who had seen her devastation when she'd come home from Italy. Her father hadn't even noticed, and had barely acknowledged her pregnancy in his sheer self-absorption. When Milo had appeared her father had merely raised an eyebrow and proceeded to behave as if he'd always been there.

Sam reached out and took Bridie's hand, squeezing it. 'I'm glad you're here.'

'So am I, love,' Bridie said, and then with obvious glee, 'I'm going to meet the Pope!'

Sam laughed, 'I know Rafaele can do most things, but I'm not sure his influence extends to that.'

'Not sure my influence extends to what?'

Sam tensed and looked up to catch Rafaele's green gaze. She blushed and said, 'Nothing... Milo should eat now. He'll be hungry.'

Bridie stood up and took Milo from Rafaele. 'I'll have a word with the stewardess and we'll get him sorted.'

Rafaele sat down in Bridie's vacant seat when they were gone and extended his long legs into the aisle. He was the epitome of Italian masculine elegance today, in a dark grey suit, white shirt and tie. But all Sam could think of was the raw magnetism lurking under the surface of that urbanity.

'It's rude to talk about people behind their backs, you know,' he observed without rancour.

Sam was immediately suspicious of this more civil Rafaele. He was undoubtedly happy to be returning to his own milieu.

She smiled tightly and avoided his gaze. 'Don't worry. Your number two fan only has good things to say about you.'

'Unlike you...'

In a bid to break the sudden tension Sam asked quickly, 'Your father...he knows about us coming?'

Rafaele sat back a little further. Milo could be heard chattering happily further up the plane.

The reserve that came over Rafaele's features at the mention of his father didn't go unnoticed by Sam.

'I spoke to him on the phone and explained.'

'How did he take the news of...of a grandson?'

Rafaele's mouth thinned. 'He's looking forward to meeting the next generation.'

'You're not close to him, are you?'

Rafaele looked at her and asked almost accusingly, 'How do you know?'

She shrugged minutely. 'You never spoke about him much…and I know you didn't grow up with him.'

'No,' he conceded. His mouth was even thinner, making Sam want to reach out and touch him. She curled her hands into fists in her lap.

With evident reluctance he said, 'My mother left him when I was three and took me with her. He was in no state to care for me even if she'd wanted to leave me behind.'

In an instant Sam remembered the day they'd told Milo who Rafaele was and Rafaele had made that enigmatic comment about being three years old. He must have been referring to this.

'Your mother wouldn't have done that, surely…?'

Rafaele arched a dark brow. 'No? So why did she abandon my older half-brother? Her firstborn son?'

Sam's mouth opened and closed. 'You have another brother?'

As if regretting saying anything, Rafaele said briskly, 'He turned up out of the blue at my mother's funeral. Alexio and I had no idea he even existed… Well, I had a memory of meeting him briefly when I was small but I thought it had been a dream.'

Half to herself, Sam said, 'So Milo has two uncles…'

Rafaele emitted a curt laugh. 'Don't worry, it's not likely we'll be getting together as one big happy family any time soon. Alexio is busy running his empire and Cesar wants nothing to do with us.'

Just then Milo came running down the aisle and grabbed Rafaele's hand, pulling him out of the seat. 'Lunch is ready!'

Rafaele let himself be pulled up and held out a hand to Sam.

She felt unsettled and a little vulnerable after their conversation. It was another snippet Rafaele hadn't revealed before. She put her hand into his and let him pull her out of the seat. He held it tightly all the way to the other end of the plane but Sam didn't feel as if the gesture was meant to be romantic. On the contrary—it was meant to remind her that they had unfinished business.

Rafaele's *palazzo* was as she remembered it: imposing, beautiful and impressive. The lush green gardens were stunningly landscaped. Its faintly crumbling grandeur hid opulent luxury inside. Four years ago Rafaele had still been in the process of doing it up and now it was finished.

As they approached up the grand steps Sam didn't even notice how tense she'd become until Milo said plaintively, 'Ow Mummy, too *tight*.' She immediately relaxed her grip on his hand.

A different housekeeper from the one Sam remembered met them at the door and Rafaele introduced her as Luisa. She was soon busy directing the driver with their bags. Bridie was open-mouthed with shock and awe, and Sam felt a semi-hysterical giggle rise up, but it faded fast when she saw the stooped figure of a man with a cane approach them.

He barked out something in Italian and Sam saw Rafaele tense just a few feet ahead of her. She had that disturbing urge again to touch him, to offer some comfort.

He said curtly, 'In English, Papa. They don't speak Italian.'

The old man snorted and came into view. His eyes were deep set and so dark they looked black, staring out from a strong face lined with age and disappointment.

Milo was clutching Sam now and she lifted him up.

'Well?' Umberto growled. 'Where is my grandson?'

Hesitantly Sam moved forward to stand beside Rafaele. She felt him snake an arm around her waist and didn't like the way something within her immediately welcomed and gravitated towards the support.

'Papa, this is Samantha Rourke, our son Milo, and Sam's friend Bridie.'

Our son.

Sam nodded in the man's direction. His black gaze seemed to be devouring them. He said nothing. Then, to Sam's complete surprise, Milo squirmed to be set free and she had to put him down.

Holding her breath, Sam watched as Milo started to walk towards his grandfather. She wanted to snatch him back, as if from the jaws of danger, and even moved. But Rafaele's hand stopped her, gripping her waist, making her *über*-aware of his hard body alongside hers. Even now...

Milo stopped in front of the man and asked with all the innocence of a child, 'Why do you have a stick?'

The man just looked at him for a long moment and then barked out a laugh. '*Dio*, Rafaele, it's like looking at you when you were that age. He's a Falcone—no doubt about it.'

Rafaele's hand gripped her waist so tightly now that Sam looked at him, but she could only see his hard jaw, a muscle twitching. Before she could do or say anything Rafaele had let her go and strode over to crouch down near Milo, who curled into him trustingly.

Huskily he was saying, 'This is your grandpapa, *piccolino*.'

Umberto Falcone held out a hand to his grandson. 'I am pleased to meet you.'

Milo grinned and took his hand, shaking it forcefully, making Umberto wince comically. Milo giggled and looked at Rafaele. 'Can we play now?'

Rafaele stood up, still holding onto Milo's hand, and something tense seemed to pass from him to his father. He said to Milo, 'Why don't we settle in first, hmm? We can play later.'

'Okey-dokey.' Milo took his hand from Rafaele's and came back to Sam, who picked him up again.

Rafaele was now drawing her and Bridie forward to introduce them to Umberto, but gone was the joking man of moments ago. He seemed to have retreated again.

Bridie was saying politely, 'You have a beautiful home here, Mr Falcone.'

The old man glanced at his son and said stiffly, 'It's not mine...it's Rafaele's. He bought it back after—'

'Papa,' Rafaele said warningly, and the man's mouth shut.

He looked at Bridie then and said, 'Come, let us take some refreshments and leave these young ones to settle in.'

Bridie looked at Sam, and Sam noticed that she was a bit pink in the cheeks. Sam pushed her gently in the direction where Umberto was setting off, surprisingly agile despite his cane and stooped figure. 'Go on—sit down and have a rest. We'll be fine.'

The housekeeper was despatching a younger woman in the direction of Umberto and Bridie with rapid Italian before leading them up the stairs herself. Sam was clinging onto Milo, afraid of the onslaught of memories lurking around each corner. She and Rafaele had made love all over this *palazzo*. He'd used to bring her here after work, apart from a couple of times when he'd taken her to her apartment, too impatient to wait, but she'd never spent a weekend here with him until that last weekend...

They were walking down a familiar corridor now, and Sam's heart thumped hard when she recognised Rafaele's bedroom door to the left. Thankfully they stopped at another door, just opposite.

'This is your room. Milo is in an adjoining one.'

Sam walked into the room indicated by Rafaele. The housekeeper disappeared. Milo wriggled to be free and she put him down so he could explore. The room was sumptuous without being over the top. Understated luxury. Lots of discreet flower designs and soft greys. Sam heard a squeal of excitement from Milo and followed him into his room.

It was a small boy's paradise. His bed was made in the shape of a car. The walls were bright. Books and toys covered almost every available surface. Sam looked at Rafaele helplessly as Milo found a toy train set.

He grabbed it up and went to Sam, 'Is this mine, Mummy?'

Sam shot Rafaele a censorious look. She bent down. 'Yes, it is, sweetie. But this is Rafaele's house. You'll have to leave it behind when we go home.'

Milo looked perturbed and turned to Rafaele. 'Will you mind it for me when we go home?'

Rafaele sounded gruff. 'Of course, *piccolino*.'

Milo's lip quivered. Sam could see that it was all too much.

'But…but what if another little boy comes and wants to play with it?'

Rafaele bent down and looked Milo in the eye. 'That won't happen. You are the only little boy who is allowed to play here, I promise.'

Instantly reassured, Milo spun away to start playing again.

Sam hissed at Rafaele. 'This is too much for him. You can't *buy* his affection, Rafaele.'

Rafaele stood up and took Sam's arm, leading her out of earshot. 'Damn you, Sam, I'm not trying to buy him… I want to spoil him—is that so bad?'

Sam looked into Rafaele's eyes and felt herself drowning. She knew instinctively that Rafaele had done this out of the generous good of his heart, *not* out of any manipulative desire. He might do that with her, but all along he'd been ultra-careful to take her lead on how to deal with Milo.

She crossed her arms and felt like a heel. She looked down. 'I'm sorry…that wasn't entirely fair.'

Rafaele tipped her chin up. 'No, it wasn't.'

All Rafaele could see were those swirling grey depths, sucking him down and down to a place he didn't want to investigate. Like Milo feeling overwhelmed, he suddenly felt the same. Letting go of Sam's chin, he stepped back. He needed space. Now.

'I'll have Luisa bring you up some refreshments. You and Milo should settle in and rest. We'll eat at seven.'

When he reached his study on the ground floor he closed the door and took a deep breath. He headed straight for his drinks cabinet and poured himself a shot of whisky, downing it in one. To his chagrin it wasn't even Milo and the fact that he had his son in this house that seemed to be featuring prominently in his head. It was Sam. Having Sam back here. Reminding him of the heated insanity he'd felt around her before. Of how badly he'd needed her, how insatiably.

How sweet she'd been—so innocent. So bright. So unlike any other woman he'd known, seducing him effortlessly into a tangled web of need from which he'd only extricated himself with great effort. And he had been relieved to do so, no matter what the dull ache he'd felt for four years might have told him.

The ache had disappeared as soon as he'd decided that he'd contact her in England. He'd told himself that it would be different, that he wouldn't still desire her. That he would be able to demonstrate how he'd moved on… But even at the first sound of her voice on the end of the phone his body had convulsed with need…

And then…*Milo*.

Rafaele felt pain lance his hand and looked down stupidly to see that he'd crushed the delicate glass. Cursing himself, he got a tissue and told himself he was being ridiculous. Seeing Sam here again, with his father too, in this *palazzo*…it was something he'd never expected to have to deal with. That was all.

The following morning when Sam woke up she was disorientated for a few long seconds, until the opulent surroundings and softer-than-soft bed registered. She sat up in a panic.

Milo.

Quickly she got out of bed and went to the open adjoining door. Milo's bed was tossed, his pyjamas were on the ground and he was nowhere to be seen.

Bridie must have taken him for breakfast. The previous evening had seen them all seated for dinner—Milo sitting on big books on a chair to elevate him, insisting on feeding himself like a big boy, wanting to impress his new grandpapa, who had looked on approvingly.

To Sam's relief, after dinner Rafaele, far too disturbing in jeans and a black top, had made his excuses and disappeared to his study. And then Bridie had insisted on taking Milo up to bed, as he'd been barely able to keep awake long enough to feed himself his new favourite dessert: *gelato.*

Sam had felt awkward, sitting with Umberto on her own, but the man had stood up and indicated for her to follow him and have some coffee, so she had. He'd led her to a small room off the dining room—comfortable, cosy.

Luisa had come and poured them coffee and Sam had felt she needed to break the ice. 'I'm sorry…that you didn't know about Milo before now.'

The old man had waved her words aside and admitted gruffly, 'I gave up any right to pry into Rafaele's life a long time ago.'

Not knowing how to respond, Sam had just taken a sip of coffee. She'd always loved the strength and potency of well-made Italian coffee.

'Milo is the same age as Rafaele was when he left here with his mother.'

Sam had looked at Umberto.

'He was very young.' The old man's face had darkened. 'Too young to witness what he did.'

Sam had frowned. 'I'm sorry… I don't know…'

Umberto had looked at her, his gaze shrewd. 'When my wife left me, Samantha, I was a broken man. I'd already lost everything. My house, the family legacy, the factory. My dignity. I begged her on my knees not to leave me but she did anyway. Rafaele witnessed my lowest moment and I don't think he's ever forgiven me for it.'

Sam had tried to take it in. She'd known Rafaele's mother had left, but not the extent of it. She wondered how traumatic it must have been for a child to see his mother turn her back on his father and it was as if something slid home inside her—she could see now where Rafaele's intensely commitment-phobic issues might stem from.

'It was a long time ago…' Umberto had said. 'It's good that you are here with Milo. This will be a challenge for my proud son, and perhaps that's not a bad thing.'

Sam blinked in the morning light of her bedroom, the memory fading. She remembered now that she'd had disjointed dreams all night of a man on his knees, begging, pleading, with Milo looking on, crying in distress… She pursed her lips. One thing she could guarantee pretty categorically was that Rafaele would never be reduced to begging on his knees to *anyone*.

Trying not to think of that vulnerable three-year-old Rafaele, when all she could see was Milo in her mind's eye, Sam washed and dressed and went to search for Milo and Bridie. She found them in the dining room with the sun pouring in.

Sam bent to kiss her son, aware of a cool green gaze on her from the head of the table. Umberto and Bridie broke off from their conversation to greet Sam and Rafaele stood up. Sam had to quell a dart of hurt. She felt as if the minute she entered a room he wanted to leave it.

'I've got to go to the factory this morning for my meeting… I've arranged for a driver to come and pick you all up in an hour. He will drop Umberto off at the doctor's and take you into Milan to sightsee. I'll join you there this afternoon for a late lunch.'

Umberto muttered something rude about doctors and Sam saw Bridie smile.

Milo was asking Sam, 'What's *sightsee?*'

Rafaele had pinned Sam with that unreadable gaze and instantly she felt breathless. 'I have to go to a function this evening. I'd like it if you accompanied me.'

Sam opened her mouth. 'I…'

Bridie chipped in quickly. 'Of course she will. You could do with a night out, Sam, love. I'll be here, and Milo can sleep with me so you won't have to worry about disturbing him.'

Sam glared at Bridie, who looked back at her with an innocence she didn't trust for a second. Umberto was unhelpfully silent.

Sam looked at Rafaele and was loath to let him see that she might not want to go for very personal reasons.

She shrugged a shoulder. 'Sure—why not?'

CHAPTER EIGHT

THAT EVENING SAM realised a fundamental flaw in her plan to join Rafaele for his function. She had no dress. She hadn't even thought about it earlier, while in Milan, too caught up in the whistlestop sightseeing tour Rafaele had arranged for Bridie and Milo, who obviously hadn't been there before. Then they'd picked Umberto up from the doctor's and met Rafaele for lunch.

Biting her lip and wondering what to do, Sam went to the wardrobe, fully expecting it to be empty. When she opened the door, though, she gasped and her heart stopped cold in her chest. There was a dress hanging up inside, and it was the dress Rafaele had bought her four years before. She remembered the big white box it had come in, along with the matching underwear, shoes and jewels. She'd left it all behind at the *palazzo* because she'd felt as if it had never really belonged to her.

About two months after Sam had returned to England the box containing the dress, shoes, underwear and jewellery had arrived via a courier company. As soon as she'd realised what it was and had read the accompanying note— *I bought this for you. Rafaele*—Sam had sent it back with the note torn in two pieces.

And now it was here.

Sam felt short of breath. She took the dress out of the wardrobe, its material heavy and slinky, and stalked out of her bedroom and across the hall to Rafaele's, not bothering to knock on the door.

Her eyes widened when she took in a naked Rafaele, strolling out of his bathroom and rubbing his hair with a towel. For a long moment he just stood there, and Sam's eyes were glued to that broad, magnificent chest. Instant heat bloomed in her belly.

With a strangled sound she lifted her eyes and held the dress out. 'What is the meaning of this?'

With supreme nonchalance Rafaele secured the towel around his waist and quirked his mouth sexily on one side. 'It's amazing how you can still blush, *cara*.'

Sam gritted out, 'Don't call me that. I'm not your *cara*. Why do you still have this dress?'

Rafaele's face was inscrutable. He shrugged. 'It seemed a shame to throw it away just because you didn't want it.'

Bile rose inside Sam. 'And how many lucky women have worn it since me?'

A muscle popped in Rafaele's jaw. 'None. I thought you'd appreciate blending in with the crowd tonight instead of appearing in your habitual tomboy uniform.'

To Sam's disgust she felt tears prick her eyes. 'I'll try not to disappoint you, Rafaele. After all, I know what an honour it is to be taken out in public with you, because you never deemed it appropriate before.'

She whirled around and left the room, slamming the door behind her.

Rafaele winced and put his hands on his hips. His chest was a tight ball of blackness. He cursed himself. He should have followed his head and thrown that dress out as soon as he'd realised she'd left it behind—instead of sending it to her, almost intrigued as to how she might respond when even then he'd known that he couldn't have anything more to do with her.

When it had arrived back with the torn note, *then* he

should have thrown it out. But instead he'd instructed his housekeeper to hang it up and had refused to analyse why he'd done such a thing.

It was just a dress.

Thoroughly disgruntled now, and regretting the impulse he'd had earlier to ask Sam to accompany him this evening, Rafaele got dressed.

Sam was still tight-lipped in the back of one of Rafaele's chauffeur-driven cars about an hour later. She was as far away from him as she could get without falling out of the door, and she hated the electric awareness that pulsed between them.

As they'd been leaving Milo had been holding Umberto's hand in the grand hallway of the *palazzo* and he'd gasped. 'Mummy, you look like a princess.'

Sam had gone red, and then grown even hotter when Rafaele had appeared, looking stupendously gorgeous in a classic tuxedo. Suddenly she'd been glad of the effort she'd made. She needed all the armour she could muster.

Her hair was up in a topknot, held in place with a jewelled pin loaned to her by Bridie. She'd put on more make-up than she'd normally wear, outlining her eyes and thickening her lashes. And wearing the vertiginous heels that had come with the dress Sam reached to Rafaele's shoulder.

He hadn't touched her while they were leaving. He'd merely indicated that she should precede him and, feeling horribly exposed under his cool gaze, Sam had walked out, praying she wouldn't fall over.

Now they were pulling up outside the glittering façade of a building with men in uniforms waiting to assist all the guests in their finery. Butterflies swarmed into Sam's belly.

She felt her arm being taken in a warm grip and showers of electric shocks seemed to spread through her body. Reluctantly she looked at Rafaele, and the momentarily unguarded look on his face took her by surprise.

'I should have told you earlier... You look beautiful.'

'I...' Sam's voice failed. 'Thank you.'

And just like that she felt the animosity drain away. She realised that as soon as she'd seen the dress hanging up she'd harboured a very treacherous wish that Rafaele had kept it for sentimental reasons, and that was the basis for her lashing out at him. It had been anger at herself for her own pathetic weakness.

Rafaele had let her go. Sam's door was being opened and someone was waiting for her to step out. When she did so, Rafaele was standing there, his face unreadable again. She wondered if she had imagined what he'd just said...

He took her arm and led her inside and Sam was glad he was supporting her, because nothing could have prepared her for the dazzling display of wealth and beauty as soon as they walked in.

She felt instantly gauche: both underdressed and overdressed. Rafaele got them drinks and almost immediately was surrounded by gushing acolytes—a mixture of men and women. As they stood there the number of women seemed to increase. They shot Sam glances ranging from the curious to the downright angry—as if he had no right to come here with a woman.

Clearly Rafaele was a prize to be fought over, and Sam really didn't like the way her own hackles rose and her blood started to boil in response. She felt a very disturbing primal urge rise up within her to claim him in some way. The fact that she had borne his child seemed to resonate deep within her, and she wanted to snarl at the women to back off.

With a lazy insouciance that did nothing to help cool her blood, Rafaele reached out and drew her to his side. The level of malevolence coming from the women increased exponentially.

He said to the people surrounding them, 'I'd like to introduce you to Samantha Rourke.'

Something in Sam went cold at this very bare introduction, which left her in some kind of limbo land—what exactly *was* she to him?

But what had she expected him to say? *Meet the mother of my child, who is such a pushover that she lets me sleep with her even though she knows I hate her...?*

Sam caught one or two smug looks from a couple of the women. As if to say, *She's no competition.* Her blood boiled over.

She managed to keep it together until they were alone again and then she rounded on him. 'If you brought me here just to deflect the attention from those man-eaters then I think I've done my bit. I'd prefer to be at home with Milo than to witness your simpering fan club line up to tell you how marvellous you are.'

Furious at herself for feeling so emotional, Sam stabbed Rafaele's chest with a finger. 'I'm the mother of your child—tell *that* to your next prospective mistress.'

Rafaele looked at Sam and felt something pierce his chest. Her words were lost to him for a second in the glare from those grey eyes. She looked so young, so stunning. Her neck was long and graceful, her skin so pale he could see the delicate veins underneath. The dress hugged and emphasised every curve, fitting her better now than it had four years ago. His eyes dropped down over the swell of her breasts and her words resounded within him: *I'm the mother of your child.*

Moments ago, when he'd reached out to pull her to him and introduce her, he'd felt a second of blind panic. The realisation had been immediate and stark: he'd just introduced his peers to Sam and when the news emerged of his son, and that she was his mother, they would assume that they were together. And that thought wasn't making him want to flee.

Rafaele had not even considered this prospect when he'd asked Sam to the function. He'd just looked at her that morning and the words had spilled out… Proving once again how she scrambled his thought processes. How she effortlessly tapped into something deep and instinctive within him that led to choices and decisions that his head might normally balk at.

He couldn't even blame her. It wasn't as if she'd inveigled her way to an invitation—if anything she'd looked horrified at the suggestion. Rafaele's blood simmered. He felt the imprint of Sam's finger in his chest. The rest of the room died away and he saw only her. Need and desire rose up to strangle him and magnified his feeling of exposure.

Reaching out a hand, he snaked it around her neck and brought her closer. Something triumphant moved through him when he saw those eyes flare with awareness. But the realisation of how comfortable he was with people knowing who Sam was, assuming they were together, was too raw, too new. He needed to push it back. Push *her* back.

'I have the only mistress I need right here, Sam. Why would I go looking when you've already proved yourself so amenable?'

Her cheeks went white and Rafaele felt the punch of something dirty and dark down low.

'You bastard.'

She pulled away from him and spun around, moving through the crowd. It was a long second before Rafaele could function again, and then he set off after her, a dense darkness expanding in his chest when he thought of those huge eyes and the pain in their depths that he'd just witnessed. That he'd just caused. Wilfully. From weakness.

* * *

Sam could barely drag enough oxygen into her lungs. She was seething. Hurt and angry with herself for letting Rafaele get to her. For feeling so possessive and jealous around those other women. For ever hoping even for a second that his bringing her here tonight had meant something…

She raised a hand to get the doorman's attention, to ask him to call her a cab, but just then it was caught by a firm grip and she was whirled around.

'Where do you think you're going?'

Rafaele looked as livid as she felt, and he had no right to be. Sam pulled her arm free. 'I'm going home, Rafaele. I don't need to be reminded publicly how little you like to acknowledge me in your life.'

She turned around again, but gave a gasp of dismay when she saw Rafaele's chauffeur-driven car stopping at the foot of the steps. He was marching her down to the open door before she could do anything. The door was quickly shut and he was sliding in the other side. Sam had a perverse urge to open the door and jump out but she curbed the childish desire. And also she realised she didn't have enough money for a cab. She scowled at herself. Being with Rafaele was eroding her very independence.

Rafaele issued a terse instruction to the driver and the privacy window slid up noiselessly. His eyes glittered at her in the gloom of the backseat but even now Sam's muscles clenched in her pelvis, and she felt the betraying heat of desire getting her body ready for this man. *Her man.* The stupid assertion flashed again. She could have growled with frustration.

Eventually he bit out, 'I shouldn't have said what I did back there. You didn't deserve that.'

It was the last thing Sam had expected to hear, and she said faintly, 'No, I didn't.' And then, 'Why did you bring me with you, Rafaele? People will only ask questions…

when they find out about Milo… We shouldn't be seen together. It doesn't help matters.'

Rafaele's face looked as if it was carved out of stone. 'You're the mother of my child, Samantha. It's inevitable that we'll be seen together, no matter what happens in the future.'

Sam had an image then of Rafaele, married to some cool blonde beauty, and of an older Milo heading off on a plane on his own to stay with his father and his new family. The image made her suck in a breath of pain and she scooted as far away from him in the back of the car as she could.

Mixed in with the pain she was feeling was the ever-present and building sexual frustration. She felt as if she was going mad. Heat burned her insides and made her skin prickle. All she could see in her peripheral vision was the huge dark shape of Rafaele and imagined that powerful body, naked and surging into hers, thrusting so deep that she'd finally feel some measure of peace.

She had to hold back a groan, and was aware of Rafaele's quick glance at her through the thick tension between them.

Lord. It had been a long time since Sam had had to pleasure herself, but if this need wasn't assuaged soon she'd go mad.

'Sam.'

Rafaele's voice was thick and Sam's heart palpitated. Reluctantly she looked at him and a pulse throbbed between her legs. She clamped her thighs together desperately.

He reached over and took her hand and Sam almost cried out at the sensation. She tried to pull back but he wouldn't release her.

'I want you.'

His face was in shadow but she could sense his desperation. It was little comfort. Inevitability rose up inside her. She could resist anything but this declaration. This promise that soon, if she allowed it, he would ease this ache that was inside her, tearing her apart. It transcended even what had just happened.

Helplessly, in a whisper of supplication that she hated, Sam just replied, 'Yes...'

Yes.

Rafaele felt primal satisfaction rush through him, hardening his body. He wanted to devour Sam, consume her, brand her. He wanted her *for ever*.

No!

Rafaele rejected that rogue assertion, which had slid into his mind before he'd even acknowledged it.

He couldn't let her hand go, though, even when she turned her head away to look out of the window. The rapid rise and fall of her breasts beneath the dress made him curl his other hand to a fist, just to stop himself reaching out to cup their heavy weight.

Sam was clearly aware of the same ramifications as he, of being seen together and how that might be construed. But the thought of her rejecting that suddenly made him want to claim her. In any way that he could. Publicly *and* in private.

But right now he couldn't really focus on what that meant. Right now he wanted the physical.

As the car swept gracefully through the *palazzo* gates anticipation spiked like a fever in his blood. When the car came to a halt he got out and strode around to Sam's door, helping her out himself. She looked up at him with those huge expressive eyes and desire was hot and urgent inside him—part of the tangled mess of emotions this woman inspired in him on a regular basis.

With one smooth move he picked her up into his arms. Her mouth was tight with a need that resonated within him.

He felt like a beast. He couldn't speak. What he needed right now was not something he could even articulate. It was visceral, physical. Urgent.

Sam was in Rafaele's arms and he was striding through the front door of the *palazzo*. All she could feel was her breasts crushed to the solid wall of his chest and the pulse of awareness between them, like a tangible forcefield of energy.

The house was quiet. He was striding up the stairs now and Sam bit her lip. Rafaele carried her straight into his bedroom. She tensed against the leap of her blood at the promise of satisfaction. A moment of sanity intruded, reminding her of the certain self-recrimination she would face in the aftermath and all the uncertainty about how he felt about her.

Weakly she seized on the first thing she thought of. 'Wait… Milo…'

Rafaele was putting her down, sliding her along the length of his hard body, one part of which in particular was very hard. He was already pulling down the strap of her dress and her skin tingled.

His voice was rough. 'Milo is with Bridie, as you well know.'

That sliver of sanity compelled her to try again, even though every part of her protested. 'Rafaele…'

'Stop talking, Sam. I want you. You want me. It's very simple.'

It *wasn't* that simple, though, and Sam opened her mouth to protest again. But then Rafaele was kissing her, and pulling the strap of her dress down further, and she felt the rising lust suck her under and weakly…she gave in. She wanted to forget sanity and take *this*.

Between her legs she was slick and throbbing. She didn't have a hope of resisting when Rafaele bared one breast and cupped it in his hand, squeezing the plump flesh, his thumb grazing her nipple.

Letting out a soft moan halfway between frustration at her own weakness and excitement at her building desire, Sam wound her arms around Rafaele's neck and pressed herself against him, trapping his hand on her breast.

Rafaele's other hand came down and cupped her buttocks, kneading the flesh, making Sam's hips roll against him impatiently. She could feel the thick length of his erection between them and fresh heat pulsed to her core.

Rafaele pulled back for a moment, breathing harshly, his eyes glittering fiercely. It was hard for Sam to open her eyes. She felt dazed. He'd always had this effect on her—one touch and she felt drugged.

He was dragging off his jacket, tie and shirt, dropping them to the ground, unbuckling his belt, undoing his trousers.

His voice was guttural. 'I want you naked *now*.'

Sam's flesh prickled with anticipation. Her hands felt stupid as she tried to pull down her strap and, issuing something that sounded like a curse, Rafaele took over, turning her around and finding the zip, pulling it down and peeling the heavy fabric from her body.

Sam kicked off her shoes. Now she wore only black lace panties. Rafaele turned her around again and that hot green gaze swept down her body, lingering on her breasts, which seemed to swell and tighten under his look.

'You're so beautiful.'

Sam ducked her head. 'No, I'm not.'

Rafaele tipped up her chin, forcing her to look at him. 'Yes, you are.'

He'd done this before—made her feel buoyant. Feminine. And it had all been ripped to pieces when he'd rejected her. But Sam couldn't focus on that now.

He pulled her into him again and Sam swayed towards

him like a magnet. He kissed her, tongue thrusting deep, fanning the flames of lust within her. He was naked now, and her hand instinctively sought to touch him, finding and encircling his erection, moving up and down, feeling the slip and slide of satin skin over all that steely strength.

His mouth not leaving hers, Rafaele skimmed his hand down from her breast over her belly, down to her panties and underneath, his fingers seeking and finding that sweet molten spot, making her legs part so that he could have more access.

As he stroked and explored Sam broke off the kiss. And then one of Rafaele's fingers thrust inside her and Sam's legs went weak with the sharp, spasming pleasure that gripped her.

With dextrous hands Rafaele pushed her panties down and lifted her, to deposit her on the bed. Sam could only look up at Rafaele and marvel at his sheer masculine magnificence. He was so broad and powerful. Narrow waist and hard-muscled thighs and between them... Her mouth watered.

She sat up and looked up at Rafaele. He was watching her almost warily and she felt a heady rush of power. She moved to the edge of the bed and reached for him, her hands going to his hips, pulling him towards her.

'Sam...'

She ignored him and drew his length into her hand, and then she took him into her mouth. The remembered taste and feel of him was like an explosion on her senses. She barely heard his deep moan of satisfaction as she swirled her tongue around the bulbous tip, relearning his shape and what made him tense. His hands were in her hair, gripping her head.

Her hand encircled him and her mouth and tongue licked and sucked. *He'd* taught her how to do this.

'*Dio*, Sam...'

Sam felt him tensing, the instinctive thrusting of his hips towards her, as if he couldn't help himself. His hands were trying to pull her back, but she knew it was against his will. He'd never let her go this far before but stubbornly Sam wanted to see him lose control because of *her* and she kept going, ignoring his rough entreaties, until finally she felt the heat of his climax gush into her mouth and throat, felt his hips jerking.

Sam kept her mouth on him for a long moment and then finally pulled back. She couldn't help a smile when she saw Rafaele's dazed-looking expression. Slowly that expression cleared and his eyes narrowed on her. She felt a shiver of trepidation mixed with anticipation go through her and recognised that he wasn't happy with the way she'd made him lose it like that. She felt more powerful in that moment than she'd ever felt...

Rafaele bent down and loomed over her on his hands, forcing her to move back onto the bed. She collapsed onto it.

'I think I'm going to have to restrain you...'

Sam looked at Rafaele blankly for a second, and then watched him stand up and go to a nearby cabinet. He pulled out two long slivers of silk and she realised they were ties. Something deep inside her quivered—but it wasn't with fear, it was excitement. She didn't know what he intended but secretly wanted to find out...

He took each hand and quietly wound a tie around each wrist, knotting it. Sam looked at him and bit her lip. Then Rafaele stretched her hands over her head, and Sam only realised what he'd done when she couldn't bring her hands down again...he'd tied them to one of the bed's four posts.

'Rafaele... What...?'

He came back down and over her. Not touching her, but letting her feel his body heat. 'I want you to know what it feels like to lose control...'

Sam could have laughed. She lost control every time she looked at this man! And there was something that felt so wickedly decadent about being restrained it overshadowed the sliver of discomfort. She trusted Rafaele above anything else, and that deep-seated knowledge shook her now. She hadn't realised just how much she trusted him till this moment.

He bent his head then, and his mouth was a hot brand on hers, opening her up to him, demanding a response which she gave unerringly. Already she felt the frustration of being bound. She wanted to touch him but couldn't. She moaned softly with it, and could have sworn she heard Rafaele chuckle darkly.

His mouth moved down, trailing over her jaw and neck. His hands were smoothing over her body, touching her but staying away from erogenous zones, making her grit her jaw to stop herself from begging. Her hands pulled ineffectually at the silken ties.

And then Rafaele's mouth was on her breast and her back arched. *Yes.* He lavished both taut peaks with attention until they were tingling and stinging. His hand had moved down to her belly and, like a wanton, Sam felt her legs part in mute appeal. Rafaele reared back for a moment and looked at her body. Sam gazed down to see his arousal already hard again, still glistening wetly from her mouth and tongue. She ached inside.

Rafaele's hand went to the juncture at her legs and then he was moving down, his mouth leaving little trails of fire as he pressed kisses under her breasts, to her abdomen and down. Sam's breath stopped when she felt him pull her legs wide apart. Her hands pulled at the ties. She'd never been so bared or so vulnerable.

Rafaele's mouth settled *there*, between her legs, and Sam's breath came back, choppy. She felt too hot, too tight, too…sensitive.

'Rafaele...'

But his tongue was on her now, exploring her sex, finding where she was so wet for him, opening her up, stabbing deep, making her moan uncontrollably, making her hips twitch. And then his tongue was replaced by his fingers, thrusting deep, and his other hand had found her breast, his thumb and forefinger pinching a nipple.

A broken scream emerged from Sam's mouth—a feral sound. Her hips were lifting off the bed, begging Rafaele for more, for him to drink from her as she came...as she'd done to him. And then the pleasure was peaking and spiralling out of all control, wresting her sane mind from her brain and leaving behind nothing but heat and deep, boneless satisfaction, with his mouth on her right to the end.

Rafaele slowly came up and over her body. He pressed a kiss to her mouth and Sam could taste the essence of her desire on him. Could he taste himself on her? The thought ignited new fires deep down, diminishing her need to curl up and cling onto the boneless feeling. Sam was barely aware of being restrained now. She didn't think she could have lifted her arms even if she'd wanted to.

And then Rafaele was sliding into her...deeply. Sam sucked in a breath, her eyes going wide. He looked down at her and all she could see was green. And heat. And broad shoulders damp with sweat. He moved back out... slowly. One arm came around her back, arching her into him, making one breast pout up towards him, so he bent his head and took it into his mouth, suckling fiercely as he thrust, going a little deeper, harder.

Sam gasped. It was too much. And now she *did* feel the restraints and she pulled against them. She needed to anchor herself to something. She felt as if Rafaele was going to drive her over the edge completely and she'd have nothing at all to hang onto.

But she couldn't articulate any words. Rafaele's chest against her breasts was delicious torture. The ruthless rhythm of his body in and out of hers drove her higher and higher. She could only look deep into his eyes, as if that alone could hold her to this earth.

Just at that moment something pierced her—*anger* at Rafaele, for reducing her to this mindless wanton, gasping and mute being. His powerful body was going so hard and deep now that Sam had to close her eyes, feeling as if a very secret part of herself was being bared to him in a way that she wasn't ready for.

Rafaele's voice was guttural. 'Sam, look at me.'

But she couldn't. He'd see it if she did. She'd never been laid so bare, made so vulnerable, and if she looked at him now he'd see how much she loved him—because she'd never stopped loving him. Even after all that had happened and the million reasons he'd given her for not loving him.

'No,' she said, equally guttural.

Sam heard his rough shout as he made his frustration clear, but both their bodies were locked in a primal dance now and they were equally unable to stop. They could only go on, until the tight grip of tension was shattered and they orgasmed moments after each other, Sam's body convulsing around Rafaele's thick length so hard that she could feel it. She was milking him, taking his very essence into her, and the feeling was so intense and powerful on top of this awful, excoriating vulnerability that tears pricked her eyes.

She turned her head away. Rafaele's body was still within her, pulsing, slowly diminishing. She felt a tear slip down one cheek and finally managed to find the words she hadn't been able to till now.

'Untie me Rafaele.'

She was trembling from an overload of pleasure and the revelation of just how deep her feelings for him were, still.

'Sam…'

'Just untie me.' Her voice sounded harsh to her own ears.

His hands reached up. She felt his arms and chest brush her body and she shivered convulsively against him. Even now. Deftly he undid the knots and Sam's arms were free again, her wrists sore after pulling against the restriction. Terrified that Rafaele would see her emotions bared, Sam scooted out from under him and off the bed. She grabbed the nearest covering she could find, which was his shirt, and pulled it on and walked to the door.

She heard Rafaele curse behind her and say, 'Sam, wait… Where are you—?'

But she was gone, walking blindly, on very wobbly legs, going anywhere that was away from his presence and his ability to reduce her to a melting mass of sensations and turbulent emotions. He'd wanted to dominate her and show her who was in control and he had done that beyond doubt. The eroticism of what she'd just been through felt tawdry now, as she imagined Rafaele coolly and clinically deciding how he would best show her who was boss. She had to get a grip before she faced him again.

Rafaele felt poleaxed. Self-recrimination rose upwards like bile. He would have an image burnt onto his retina for ever of Sam, with her hands bound above her head, her face turned away and a tear slipping down one cheek. He could still feel the strength of the pulsations of her body around his, and knew that it wasn't pain or discomfort that had made her turn away.

His last moment of semi-rational thought, he remembered, had been just before he'd come into Sam's mouth, his body thrusting against her, his hands holding her head so that he could— He cursed and got up off the bed, a restless jagged energy filling his body.

She'd always pushed him further than any other woman. He'd looked down at her when she'd taken her mouth from him—that wicked device of a torture more pleasurable than he could ever remember. She'd smiled at him and it had been full of something inherently feminine and mysterious... Rafaele's first insidious thought had been...Did she do that with *him?* The lover she'd taken? Had *he* been the first to experience her mouth around him, taking him in so deep that he'd not been able to pull back but had gone to the brink and over it... Had she milked him the same way?

The thought had made him see red. He'd felt exposed— far more exposed than just being naked in front of her. Vulnerable in a way he hadn't felt in a long time. It had had echoes of the past, when he recalled his mother looking at his father so dispassionately, even though he was broken, at her feet.

And suddenly Rafaele had wanted to regain control of a situation that was careening out of all control. He'd been losing it. So he'd bound her...so she couldn't touch him and make him forget again...but he'd still lost it anyway. Tying her up had only heightened the experience, making it even more erotic, compelling...and it had done nothing but highlight the fact that even while restrained she exerted a power over him that he couldn't deny.

He grabbed some clothes and pulled them on perfunctorily. Rafaele's gut felt sick as he left his room. She'd been crying. He looked in her room first, but it was dark and the bed was untouched. Then he went downstairs.

He found her in the drawing room, standing at the window through which he could see a full moon hanging low in the sky. On Sam his shirt reached down to the backs of her thighs. Her legs were long and slim underneath. She looked incredibly fragile in the voluminous white material.

'Sam...'

CHAPTER NINE

SAM'S SHOULDERS TENSED. Rafaele padded silently towards her on bare feet and she turned around, as if afraid he'd come too close. He saw a tumbler in her hand with a dark golden liquid.

She smiled and it was tight, lifted the glass towards him. 'Chin-chin.' And then she took a deep gulp, draining the glass.

He saw her cheeks flush but she made no sound. The evidence of tears was gone but her eyes looked huge, bruised.

'Sam…' He spoke through a sudden constriction in his throat. 'I'm sorry. I didn't mean to hurt you…'

'You didn't hurt me, Rafaele, I enjoyed it. You've obviously developed a kinkier side since I knew you… Was it any mistress in particular? Or is it just a sign of the times—routine sex is too boring?'

Rafaele gritted his jaw. He knew that Sam had been with him all the way because he'd felt the excitement in her body pushing him on…her distress had come afterwards…

'I've never done that with another woman,' he admitted reluctantly. He'd never felt the need to.

Sam emitted a curt laugh and raised a dark brow. 'So it's just me? I should feel flattered that I made you so angry you felt you had to restrain me…?'

Rafaele frowned, losing the thread. 'Angry?' Had it been that obvious? His fit of jealousy and vulnerability?

But Sam was continuing. 'I know you're angry about Milo, Rafaele, but you can't take it out on me like this.'

Half without thinking, Rafaele said, 'But I'm not angry about Milo.'

He realised in that moment that he truly didn't feel angry about that—not any more. It had faded and been replaced by a much darker anger…stemming from this woman's unique ability to make him lose his self-control and lose sight of what was important to him. Anger that he felt so vulnerable around her.

But Sam seemed not to have heard him. She came closer to put the empty glass down and Rafaele could see the tantalising curve of her breast through the haphazardly tied shirt. Instantly his lower body was on fire, reacting. He had a momentary revelation: *he was never going to get enough of this woman, not even in a lifetime. It would never burn out between them, only grow brighter.*

Rafaele was stunned, his head expanding with the terrifying knowledge that he would never be free of this insatiable need. He was barely aware of Sam walking out of the room. His brain was working overtime, trying to take in the knowledge that had come to him earlier, before he'd really been ready to deal with it, that he couldn't let her go. And now it was the most obvious thing in the world.

Sam gripped the bannister as she went up the stairs. Rafaele might have just said that he wasn't angry about Milo… but he *was* still angry with her. It was as clear as day. Maybe it was because he wanted her and resented himself for it?

Any control she'd clawed back before Rafaele had appeared and during that brief conversation had drained away again, leaving her feeling shaky. Somehow she got to her room, closed the door behind her and sagged against it. Tears pricked her eyes. Again. More tears for the man downstairs whom she would probably never be able to read.

Sam was too drained to deal with buttons. Her body was made weak from pleasure and sensation. She ripped Rafaele's shirt, making buttons pop and fall silently to the ground, and crawled into bed. In the morning she would shower and wash the scent of sex off her skin, but right now—treacherously—she didn't want to. In spite of what had happened.

'Rafaele said that we'll be leaving in an hour for Rome.'

Sam looked up with a studied air of nonchalance at Bridie, who had just come into the dining room. 'Oh?'

Bridie had Milo by the hand and he ran over to Sam, who picked him up and hugged him close, revelling in his sturdy body and sweet baby scent.

Bridie helped herself to some coffee and asked, 'How was the function last night?'

When Sam had woken that morning and come downstairs Bridie, Milo and Umberto had evidently already eaten, because the detritus of breakfast had been at the table but they had not. To her intense relief it appeared as if Rafaele had eaten also, as his place at the head of the table had already been used.

'It was…very swish,' Sam replied, knowing Bridie would love to hear about all the gowns and luxury. She took the cowardly way out and detailed to Bridie all of those things, while trying to ignore the disturbing memories threatening to spill into her mind at any given moment.

It took less than an hour to get from Milan to Rome and they arrived by lunchtime. Rafaele had arranged for one of his assistants to meet them at the airport with a car, and Bridie was whisked off in it to the Vatican, for the private tour Rafaele had arranged for her—much to her delight.

Another car was waiting for them, and Sam saw that Rafaele was going to drive them himself as he deftly secured Milo into the child's car seat installed in the back. It made Sam think once again of how seamlessly Rafaele had incorporated Milo into his life and her heart ached to think of what might have happened if she had told Rafaele from the start about her pregnancy.

Sam got into the car and her heart thudded heavily when Rafaele settled his powerful body behind the wheel. So far this morning she'd managed to avoid saying anything more than yes or no.

He glanced at her now and she had to acknowledge him. She turned and his gaze on her was intent. Her face grew hot as lurid images from the previous night came back.

'Okay?' he asked, disconcerting her because there was a quality to his voice she hadn't heard before. It sounded intimate. Concerned.

Sam was sure she'd imagined it so nodded quickly and looked back at Milo, who smiled, showing his small teeth. He was clutching a floppy teddy bear that Umberto had gifted him on their departure. Sam had been surprised to see what had looked suspiciously like tears in the old man's eyes as they'd left, and also a lingering glance or two at Bridie, who had looked a bit more flustered than she usually did.

As Rafaele negotiated their way out of the private airfield Sam said, 'Your father...was not what I expected.'

Rafaele's mouth tightened, but he said, 'No...I was surprised at how he welcomed Milo so instantaneously.'

'It was nice,' Sam admitted. 'After all, he's his only living grandparent now. My father was only alive to see Milo as a baby, so they didn't really connect and Milo won't remember him. Bridie is like a granny to Milo, but it's different when it's blood...'

Rafaele looked at her, his face inscrutable. 'Yes,' he agreed. 'It is.'

For the first time Sam didn't feel that Rafaele was getting in a dig. He was sounding almost as if he was realising the same thing himself.

'We should...' Sam blushed and stopped. 'That is, I should make sure to try and let Milo see Umberto as much as possible. Do you think he'd come to England?'

Rafaele's mouth quirked and he slid another glance to Sam. 'I think he could be persuaded—especially if Bridie is going to be there.'

Sam smiled, rare lightness filling her chest. 'You noticed it too, then?'

Rafaele looked at her and grew serious. He took her hand from her lap and held it. Immediately Sam's body reacted. She tried to pull away but he wouldn't let her. Memories of the bondage of last night came back. Arousing her. Disturbing her.

He said something crude in Italian and had to let Sam's hand go to navigate some hairy traffic. When it was clear again he said, 'Sam, we need to talk...'

'No,' Sam said fiercely, panicked at the thought of dissecting what had happened last night. She looked back at Milo, who was still happily playing with the toy, and then back to Rafaele. 'There's nothing to discuss.'

'Yes, there is, Sam,' he asserted, 'whether you like it or not. Tonight we'll go out for dinner.'

'Rafaele—'

But he cut her off with a stern look.

Sam shut her mouth and sat back, feeling mutinous. But deep down she knew Rafaele was right. They had to talk, but she would make sure that it would centre around the future and what would happen with Milo and also on the fact that she didn't want to sleep with him again. *Liar*, a voice mocked her. But she quashed it. Last night had almost broken her. She'd nearly revealed just how much Rafaele made her feel. And if they slept together again... she wouldn't be able to keep it in.

'I'll drop you and Milo off at the apartment and show you around, and then I'm afraid I have to go into the office for a couple of hours.'

'Okay,' Sam said, too quickly, seizing on the fact that she'd have a few hours' respite from Rafaele's disturbing presence. Maybe then these memories would abate and give her some peace.

Rafaele's Rome apartment was situated in a beautiful crumbling building just streets away from the famous Piazza Barberini, right in the heart of Rome's bustling centre. A smiling housekeeper met them and conversed easily in English for Sam's benefit. Rafaele showed Sam to her room, which was stunning, with parquet floors and delicate Rococo furnishings. There was another door which Milo was already reaching up to try and open, but the handle was too high.

He turned around, comically frustrated, and Rafaele scooped him up. 'First you have to grow a little more, *piccolino*.'

Rafaele opened the door and walked through, leaving Sam to follow them. It was a room for Milo, and once again Rafaele had obviously given instructions for it to be decked out for a three-year-old. It was a kiddie's paradise, and Milo was already jumping out of Rafaele's arms to explore all the treasures.

Rafaele looked at Sam, as if expecting another diatribe, but she could only smile ruefully and shrug her shoulders as if to say, *What can I do?*

He came closer then, blocking out Milo behind him, and cupped her jaw with a hand, his thumb rubbing her lower lip, tugging at it. Instantly Sam craved his mouth there, kissing her hard, pressing his body against hers.

Heat flooded her and she had to pull away with an effort. She shook her head, warning him off.

He said silkily, 'Tonight, Sam. We'll talk then.' He turned back to Milo. '*Ciao, piccolino.* I have to go to work now.'

Milo stopped what he was doing and for the first time since Rafaele had entered their lives, ran to him and gave him a kiss when Rafaele bent down to hug him.

'Bye, Daddy.'

Milo's easy and rapid acceptance of this whole situation made Sam's chest ache, and that emotion threatened to bubble over. She'd never in a million years envisaged that it could be this easy...or this cataclysmic.

Rafaele left and a long, shuddering breath emerged from her mouth. In truth, she'd not known what to expect if she'd ever plucked up the courage to tell Rafaele about Milo, but it had ranged from complete uninterest to his storming into their lives to take over, demand to take control.

It had definitely veered towards the latter end of the scale, but also *not*. For one thing she hadn't expected Rafaele still to want her. Or to admit that he had thought about her—that he'd never *stopped* wanting her.

Questions made her head hurt... So why had he let her go, then? If he'd wanted her...? She knew instinctively that she'd got too close. Was that why he'd pushed her away?

'Mummy, play with me!' came the imperious demand that sounded suspiciously like someone else.

Sam looked at her son and smiled. She got down on the floor beside him and devoted herself to the fantastical world of a bright, inquisitive three-year-old and welcomed the distraction.

That evening Bridie was still brimming over after her trip to St Peter's and the Vatican. 'I was the only one looking at the Sistine Chapel—the only one! And I think I saw the Pope walking in a private garden, but I couldn't be sure... A lovely priest said Mass in Latin. Oh, Sam, it was gorgeous.'

Sam smiled indulgently as she went to pick up her bag. Rafaele had called to say he was sending a car to pick her up and he'd meet her directly at the restaurant.

Suddenly Bridie broke off from her raptures and said in a shocked voice, 'You're not going out like *that?*'

Sam looked down at her outfit of jeans and a plaid shirt. Trainers. Suddenly she felt gauche. Of course Rafaele would have probably booked somewhere extremely fancy and expensive. She should have realised.

Bridie was bustling off. 'I know you packed that black dress, Sam. You have to change.'

Sam followed Bridie, knowing that she couldn't leave without changing now. Bridie seemed determined to throw her and Rafaele together, clearly believing that a fairytale ending was in the making.

When Sam walked into the bedroom Bridie was shaking out the plain black dress that Sam had packed just in case.

'Now, put this on and do your make-up. I'll let you know when the car gets here.'

Milo came barrelling down the hallway. Bridie caught him and said, 'Right, dinnertime for you, young man, and then an early night. We have to go home tomorrow so you need to be fresh.'

Sam quickly changed clothes and grimaced at her reflection, finally putting on some foundation to take away the pallor of her cheeks and then some mascara.

Home tomorrow. No wonder Rafaele wanted to talk now. He would have strong ideas about how they would proceed from here, she didn't doubt it, and she felt a shiver of trepidation that he would want to change their routine utterly.

This was all an exciting holiday to Milo now, but it couldn't continue like this. He needed routine and stability, and his life—*their* lives—were in England.

Sam heard Bridie call out, 'Sam, the car is here!'

Taking a deep breath and slipping on the one pair of low-heeled shoes she'd brought, Sam went to meet her fate.

The restaurant was nothing like Sam had expected. The car had taken her across the river to the very hip and bustling Trastevere area and the building looked small and rustic, with tables outside despite the cool early February air. Golden light spilled onto the pavement and the smells coming out of the door were mouth-watering.

Sam went in and immediately her eye was drawn to the tall man who'd stood up. Her heart kicked betrayingly, as if she hadn't seen him just hours ago. She felt ridiculously shy all of a sudden too—which was crazy, considering what had taken place in Rafaele's bedroom last night.

By the time a solicitous waiter had taken her coat and she'd made her way through the small tables to Rafaele her face was burning.

He held a chair out for her and Sam felt self-conscious in her dress, hoping that Rafaele wouldn't think she'd gone to any extra-special effort.

In a bid to deflect his attention she said quickly, 'Bridie thought I should dress up a bit...' She looked around the restaurant. 'But I don't think I needed to. I thought you might choose somewhere more upmarket.'

'Disappointed?' Rafaele's voice sounded tight.

Sam looked at him quickly and felt her hair slide over her shoulder. 'Oh, no! I love it. It's just...I never expected you to like a place like this.'

Something relaxed in Rafaele's face and seeing the faint stubbling on his jaw made Sam feel hot for a second as she imagined the abrasive rub of it between her legs. She pressed them together tightly under the table, disgusted with herself.

'This is my favourite restaurant. They specialise in cuisine from the north and they're world renowned. But they've remained humble and haven't sold out...'

Just then a man with a huge barrel chest came over and greeted Rafaele effusively, before taking Sam's hand in his and lifting it to his mouth to kiss. She couldn't help smiling, even though she couldn't understand a word he was saying. She caught *'bellissima'* and blushed, which only made him gush some more.

Eventually he left, and Rafaele indicated after him with his head. 'That's Francisco—the manager... I've known him since my student days when I used to work here.'

Sam's eyes widened as she recalled Rafaele telling her about his working three jobs to get through college. 'You worked *here?*'

He nodded and broke some bread to dip into oil and balsamic vinegar. Sam took some bread too, a little blindsided at imagining a younger, driven Rafaele working here, with women drooling over him in his waiter's uniform of white shirt and black trousers.

She admitted wryly, 'That's a little hard to believe.'

Rafaele arched a brow, mock affronted. 'You don't think I'm capable of taking orders and clearing tables?'

Sam felt a flutter near her heart and looked away, embarrassed. This was so reminiscent of before, when Rafaele had been intent on wooing her.

She looked at him. 'You never...talked about this stuff before...'

Immediately his expression closed in and Sam wanted to reach out and touch him. Her hands curled to fists.

'Before was different...'

Sam's mouth twisted and old bitterness rose up. 'I know. You didn't want to be seen in public with me.'

Rafaele looked at her, his jaw tense. 'It wasn't like that—'

A waiter interrupted them then and asked for their orders.

Another couple entered the restaurant, hand in hand, and Sam felt a bittersweet yearning rise up within her. Damn Bridie for making her wish for something that would never exist. She'd been foolish enough to hope for it in the past. She wouldn't make the same mistake again.

When the waiter had left with their menus Sam sat back and looked at Rafaele. 'What *was* it like, then?'

For a second he looked so like Milo did when he was reluctant to do something that he took her breath away and she felt tenderness fill her.

'I didn't want to share you...that's the truth. I wanted to lock you away in my *palazzo*. It used to drive me crazy that you worked all day surrounded by men who would look at you and want you.'

Sam had to bite back a strangled laugh and ignore a very treacherous swooping of her belly to hear the evident jealousy in Rafaele's voice. 'No, they didn't!'

'They did,' Rafaele growled. 'You didn't notice, though—oblivious to your effect on them. I'd never met another woman like you, and certainly not one who could match any man around her for knowledge and expertise. One who managed to turn me on more than I'd thought was possible.'

The swooping sensation intensified and Sam felt increasingly out of her depth—as if the rules had changed and she wasn't sure where she stood any more. Their starter arrived and Sam concentrated on it as if it was the most interesting thing in the world. She was in uncharted waters with Rafaele, and not sure where this conversation was headed.

After the starter was cleared Rafaele sat back and took his wineglass in his hand. Sam sensed the interest coming from a couple of women who had come in a few minutes before and, like last night, felt the rush of jealousy in her blood.

Slowly he said, 'Sam…last night at the function…'

She tensed. She really didn't want to talk about it. That acrid jealousy was all too recent and current.

'I didn't mean what I said…about you becoming my mistress. I know you're not that kind of woman.'

Sam emitted a small laugh and felt a dart of hurt. 'You can say that again.'

He leant forward and put his wine down, '*Dio*, Sam, stop putting words in my mouth. I meant that you're worth more than any other woman who was there last night.'

She looked at him and her heart jumped into her throat. His eyes were intense on hers.

With imperfect timing the waiter appeared again with their food, and Sam looked at the fish she'd evidently ordered but couldn't remember selecting now. *You're worth more than any other woman who was there.*

She looked at Rafaele and whispered, 'What do you mean?'

'Eat…then we'll talk.'

Sam felt as if she could no more eat than walk over hot coals, but she forced some of the succulent food down her throat and wished she could enjoy it more. She was sure it was delicious.

When the dishes were cleared away Sam felt very on edge. Rafaele regarded her steadily and her nerves felt as if they were being stretched taut.

Finally he clarified, 'I should have thought more about it before taking you with me last night.'

He obviously saw something Sam was unaware of on her expressive face because he put up a hand and went on, '*Not* because I don't want to be seen with you in public but because you were right. We need to know what…we are.'

Sam frowned. 'What *we* are?'

Rafaele reached out and took her hand. Sam looked at her much smaller pale hand in his dark one and her insides liquefied.

'Sam…I think we should get married.'

Sam raised her eyes to his. Shocked. 'What did you just say?'

'I said, I think we should get married.'

Sam was barely aware of Rafaele letting her hand go so that the waiter could put down coffee and dessert in front of them. She was stunned. Blindsided.

She shook her head, as if that might rearrange her brain cells into some order so that she could understand what Rafaele had just said. She had to be sure. 'Did you just say that you think we should get married?'

He nodded, looking at her carefully, as if she was made of something explosive and volatile.

'I… Why on earth would you say that?'

Now that the words were sinking in, a reaction was moving up through Sam's body, making her skin prickle. Four years ago, in the time between finding out she was pregnant and seeing Rafaele again, she'd daydreamed of such a moment—except in her dream Rafaele had been on one knee before her, not sitting across a table looking as if he'd just commented on the weather.

The most galling thing of all was that she had grown up vowing never to marry, terrified of the way her father had effectively gone to pieces after losing her mother. But she'd forgotten all about that when she'd met Rafaele, weaving dreams and fantasies around him that had had no place in reality.

'Why?' she repeated again, stronger now. Almost angry. Definitely angry, in fact. 'Do you think that I'm some kind of charity case and I'll be only too delighted to say yes because you can take care of me and Milo?'

She couldn't stop now.

'Decorating a few bedrooms doesn't a father and husband make, Rafaele. So I don't know where you're getting this notion from. It's just another way to control us, isn't it?'

His eyes flashed at her outburst. 'No, Sam. Think about it. Why *shouldn't* we get married? I've been thinking about buying a home in London. We could live there. Bridie could come too… We could look for a good school for Milo. A lot of my work for the foreseeable future will be in England, and my commutes to Europe shouldn't take me away too much…'

He had it all figured out. Square Sam and Milo away in a convenient box and tick them off the list. On the one hand the image he presented tugged at a very deep and secret part of her—a fantasy she'd once had. She only had to think of last night and how close she'd come to baring herself utterly. She didn't doubt that he hadn't factored in the reality that she would want to be a wife for *real*.

Terrified at the strength of emotion she was feeling, Sam stood up and walked quickly out of the restaurant.

Rafaele watched Sam leave. Not the first time he'd provoked her into walking away from him. She'd looked horrified. Not the reaction a man wanted when he proposed. He grimaced and acknowledged that he hadn't exactly *proposed*. But since when had Sam wanted hearts and flowers? *Did* she want that? What he was suggesting was eminently practical. Logical. Unfortunately Sam plus any attempt on his part to apply logic always ended up in disaster.

Rafaele stood up. His friend Francisco was waving him

out of the restaurant to go after his lover. The old romantic. Rafaele just smiled tightly.

When he emerged into the street it was quiet. This time of year it was mainly locals. But in a few months the place would be warm and sultry and heaving. Sam was stalking away, and when he called her she only seemed to speed up.

Cursing softly, Rafaele followed her and caught up. 'Your coat and bag, Sam.'

She stopped and turned around, arms crossed mutinously across her breasts. She reached out and grabbed for them, pulling the coat on, hitching her bag over her shoulder.

She looked at him and her eyes were huge in the gloom. 'I don't know why you would even suggest such a thing.'

Rafaele curbed his irritation. Did she really have to sound so repulsed at the idea?

He dug his hands into his pockets to stop himself from reaching for her—he didn't know if he wanted to shake her right now or kiss her. Actually, that was a lie. He'd always want to kiss her, no matter what. That thought sent shards of panic into his bloodstream.

'I happen to think it's a very good idea. There are far more reasons why you should consider this than not. We have a history. We get on well. We have a child together... And there's the physical chemistry. You can't deny that, *cara*.'

'The chemistry will burn out.'

That was said with a desperately hopeful edge that resonated within Rafaele.

He had to make her see what he'd realised last night— that marriage was the solution... *To this tangled mess of emotions you don't want to deal with*, his conscience sneered. He ignored his conscience. Surely by marrying her he would no longer experience this wildness around her? This need to devour, consume? This loss of all reason? It would negate this completely alien need to possess her… It would publicly brand her as *his*, and maybe then he'd feel some equanimity again.

'We have a child. Is that not enough of a reason? I want Milo to have my name. He is heir to a vast industry and fortune.'

'No, Rafaele,' she said in a small voice. 'It's not enough. I might have thought it would be at one time, but not any more. I want more for me and Milo. He deserves to have two parents who love each other.'

Rafaele responded with a sneering edge to his voice. 'You and I both know that fairytale doesn't exist. What we have is better than that, Sam. We can depend on each other. We respect each other.'

She lifted her chin. 'How do I know you've forgiven me for keeping Milo from you? That you won't use it in the future? That it won't be a reason for resentment when you think about it?'

Rafaele slashed a hand through the air. 'Sam, it's not about that any more. I appreciate that you had your reasons, and I admit that I didn't give you any indication to believe that I would welcome a child into my life. We can't change the past, but we can make sure we go into the future right.'

For a long moment Sam just looked at him, and then she said, 'I won't marry you. Not just to make things nice and tidy. To make things easier for you. I want more…' She shrugged her shoulder in a gesture of apology.

Rafaele felt the red mist of rage rising when he thought of some other man moving into that cosy house in the quiet suburbs, waking up next to Sam, having lazy early-morning sex…

'Do you really think someone like your ex-lover can give you a happy-ever-after? When it doesn't even exist?'

Sam started to back away. 'I'm not talking about this

any more, Rafaele. I don't want to marry you. It's plain and simple.'

Rafaele felt his chest tighten and an awful cold feeling seeped into his veins. 'Well, then...' He almost didn't recognise his own voice. 'It would appear that you're giving me no option but to take the legal route to establish custody of my son.'

Sam stopped and crossed her arms. She whispered, 'It doesn't have to come to that, Rafaele. We can come to an arrangement.'

Rafaele felt as hard inside as granite. 'I want my son, Sam, and I want him to have my name.'

'I can't fight you in a court, Rafaele. I don't have those kinds of resources.'

Rafaele pushed down his conscience. He was full of darkness—a darkness that had clung to him all his life. He was standing in front of this woman and for one second, when she'd said she didn't want to marry him, he'd been tempted to go down on one knee to convince her. It had been fleeting, but there. And it had been like a slap in the face. Had he learnt *nothing?*

Sam would not reduce him to that. No woman would. All that mattered was his son. He would not walk away from him and leave him to fend for himself as his own father had done with him.

Rafaele's voice was as cold as he felt inside. 'You're the one who started this, Samantha.'

Sam's arms tightened and Rafaele could see her knuckles turn white against the skin of her fingers.

'You were stringing us along all this time, lulling me into a false sense of security. We're leaving here tomorrow to go home. Do your worst—see if I care.'

Rafaele felt impervious to anything in that moment. He was numb. He saw Sam spot a taxi driving slowly alongside them. A very rare Rome taxi. She hailed it and jumped in. When she passed him, her profile was stony through the window. Rafaele felt something trying to break through, to pierce this numbness that had settled over him, but he pushed it down ruthlessly and tried to ignore the feeling that something very precious had just shattered into pieces.

CHAPTER TEN

THE FOLLOWING DAY Rafaele saw them off at the airport. They had been booked onto a scheduled flight home, albeit first class.

Milo was confused and kept saying, 'Why is Daddy not coming too, Mummy?'

Sam repeated for the umpteenth time, praying that she wouldn't start crying, 'Because he has to work. We'll see him again soon.' *Probably in a courtroom!* she thought half hysterically.

She'd gone straight to her bedroom last night when she'd got in, and locked the door. Not that Rafaele would be banging it down to get in. Rafaele's cold proposal had shown her that nothing had changed. He wanted Milo and he merely saw her as a way to get to him.

Once she'd said no to him he'd revealed his true colours. She felt sick to think that perhaps even the physical side of things had been a monumental act for him. Going through the motions so that he could use that as one more thing to bind them together.

Sam caught a worried glance from Bridie and forced a smile. She couldn't take Bridie's maternal inquisitiveness now. Better that she think nothing was wrong and everything was as per schedule—Rafaele had told them on the flight over that he would be staying on in Rome for work. Sam's head hurt when she thought of what would happen in the immediate future, with regard to Rafaele staying in her house.

Rafaele had Milo in his arms and was saying in a low, husky voice that managed to pluck at Sam's weak and treacherous heartstrings, '*Ciao, piccolino.* I'll see you very soon.'

Milo threw his small chubby arms around Rafaele's neck and Rafaele's eyes met Sam's over Milo's shoulder. His green gaze was as cold as ice and it flayed Sam. Their flight was called and she put her hands out for Milo. After a long moment he handed him over.

Then Bridie was saying goodbye to Rafaele, and gushing again over her trip to the Vatican, and Sam was walking away towards the gate, feeling as if her heart was being ripped to pieces.

'I thought I might stay on here for a while, if you don't mind?'

Rafaele curbed the urge to snarl at his father. It had been a week since Sam and Milo had returned home and an aching chasm of emptiness seemed to have taken up residence in his chest.

'Of course,' he said curtly. 'This is your home as much as mine.'

The old man smiled wryly. 'If it hadn't been for you it would have remained in ruins, owned by the bank.'

Rafaele said gruffly, 'That's not important. Everything is different now.'

'Yes,' Umberto said. 'Milo is…a gift. And Sam is a good woman. She is a good woman for *you*, Rafaele. Real. Honest.'

Rafaele emitted a curt laugh and said, 'Don't speak of what you don't know, Papa. She kept my son from me for nearly four years.'

Rafaele stood up from the dining table then and paced

to the window. He'd only come back to Milan to check on the factory and now he felt rootless. He wanted to go back to England to see Milo but was reluctant because… *Sam*. She brought up so many things for him.

'She must have had good reason to do so.'

Yes, she did. You gave her every reason to believe you couldn't wait to see the back of her.

Rafaele's conscience slapped him. It slapped him even harder when he thought of the resolve that had sat so heavily in his belly when he'd decided that he would have to let her go. Of her face when he'd confirmed that he didn't want to see her any more. It was the same feeling he'd had in his chest the other night in the street.

His jaw was tight as he answered his father. 'Once again, it's none of your business.'

He heard his father's chair move behind him but stayed looking out the window, feeling rigid. Feeling that old, old anger rise up even now.

'I'm sorry, Rafaele…'

Rafaele tensed all over and turned around slowly. 'Sorry for what?'

Umberto was looking at him, his dark gaze sad. 'For everything. For being so stupid as to lose control of myself, for gambling away our fortune, for losing the business. For begging your mother not to leave in front of you… I know seeing that must have had an effect…'

Rafaele smiled and it was grim, mirthless. It hid the awful tightening in his chest, which made him feel as if he couldn't draw enough breath in. 'Why did you do it? Why didn't you just let her go? Why did you have to beg like that?'

His father shrugged one shoulder. 'Because I thought I loved her. But I didn't really love her. I just didn't know it then. I wanted her because she was beautiful and emotionally aloof. By then I'd lost it all. She was the one thing left and I felt that if she went too then I'd become vapour. Nothing.'

Rafaele recalled his words as if it was yesterday. *'How can you leave me? If you leave I'm nothing. I have nothing.'*

'I wanted you, you know,' he said now in a low voice. 'I wanted to take you back when I got a job and was making a modest living. But your mother wouldn't let me near you. I was only allowed to see you on those visits to Athens.'

Rafaele remembered those painfully tense and stilted meetings. His mother had been vitriolic in her disgust at the man who had once had a fortune and had lost it, compounding Rafaele's sense of his father as a failure and compounding his own ambition to succeed at all costs.

'Why are you telling me this now?' Rafaele demanded, suddenly angry that his father was bringing this up.

'Because I can see the fear in you, Rafaele. I know that it's driven you to become successful, to build Falcone Industries from the ground up again. But you don't have to be afraid. You're not like me. You're far stronger than I ever was. And you won't do to Milo what I did to you. He will never see you weak and humiliated.'

Rafaele felt dizzy now, because he knew that he did have the capacity to repeat exactly what his father had done. He'd almost done it the other evening, albeit not in front of his son. *Thank God.*

Umberto wasn't finished, though. 'Don't let fear ruin your chance of happiness, Rafaele. I lived with bitterness for a long time and it makes a cold bedfellow. You have proved yourself. You will never be destitute… Don't be afraid to want more.'

Rafaele saw his father then, slightly hunched, his face lined with a sadness he'd never truly appreciated before.

'I'm not afraid,' he said, half defiantly. But he knew it was a lie. He realised he was terrified.

* * *

'Come on, you, it's time for bed.'

'No. Don't want to go to bed.'

Sam sighed. Milo had been acting up ever since they'd got home, and every single day he asked for Rafaele.

'Where's my daddy? When is he coming back in the car? Why can't we have a car? Where is Grandpapa?'

Sam shared a look with Bridie, who was helping to clear up Milo's things, just as the doorbell rang. They looked at each other and immediately Milo ran for the door, shrieking, *'Daddy, Daddy!'*

Sam went after him, her heart twisting. 'Milo, it won't be him…'

She pulled him back from the door and opened it, fully expecting to see just a neighbour or a door-to-door religious tout. But it wasn't either of those.

'Daddy!' Milo's small clear voice declared exactly who it was.

He was jumping up and down, endearingly still too shy to throw himself at the man who had only so recently come into his life. But when Rafaele bent down and opened his arms Milo ran straight into them and Sam's heart squeezed so tight it hurt. She heard Bridie behind her exclaim and usher Rafaele in.

Sam could see that he was holding something in his hand, and when he put Milo down he handed it to him. It was a mechanical car.

Milo seized it with inelegant haste. 'Wow!'

Sam chided him automatically through a fog of shock. 'Milo, what do you say?'

'Thank you!'

Sam was so tense she could crack. She avoided looking at Rafaele, dreading seeing that ice-cold green again.

Bridie was taking Milo by the hand and saying, 'Come

on, you promised you'd help me to find my spectacles in my flat earlier—'

Milo started protesting, and Sam felt like doing the same, but Bridie had lifted Milo up and was quelling his protests by promising him a DVD. And then they were gone before Sam could get a word out, and she was alone in the hall with Rafaele.

She still hadn't really looked him in the eye as he reached out and pushed the front door closed. Finally she looked at him and her eyes widened. He looked terrible. Well, as terrible as a gorgeous Italian alpha male *could* look—which was not terrible at all. But Rafaele looked tired, drawn, pale. Older. Somehow diminished.

Immediately Sam was concerned and said, 'What is it? Your father?'

Rafaele shook his head. 'No, it's not my father. He is fine. Asking after you all.'

'Well…what is it, then? You look…' *As bad as I feel.*

Rafaele smiled, but it was tight, and then it faded again and he'd never looked more serious.

Sam crossed her arms and started babbling out of nervousness. 'Are you here ahead of your team of lawyers? Because if you are you could have saved yourself the bother, Rafaele…'

He shook his head and looked pained. For an awful moment Sam thought there might be something wrong with *him* and she felt weak.

'No. I should never have said that to you. I'm sorry. Of course there won't be a team of lawyers…'

Sam wanted to sit down. Relief swept through her like a cleansing balm. 'But why did you say it then?'

Rafaele gave out a curt laugh. 'Because you threaten me on so many levels and I thought I could control it… control *you*.'

His words sank in. *You threaten me.* And then, as if

feeling constricted, Rafaele took off his battered leather jacket and draped it over the bottom of the stairs. He was wearing a light sweater and worn jeans and Sam could feel her blood heating. Already.

Suddenly Rafaele asked, 'Do you mind if I have a drink?'

Sam shook her head and stood back. He walked into the front room and, bemused, she uncrossed her arms and followed him. Rafaele was at the sideboard, pouring himself a shot of her father's whisky. He looked around and held up a glass in a question but she shook her head. She stood tensely inside the door. Half ready to flee.

Her voice felt rusty, unused. 'Rafaele, why are you here?'

He turned around to face her. 'Because we need to talk. Properly talk.'

Sam tensed even more, and as if sensing she was about to say something Rafaele put up a hand to quell her.

'I told you that I was about Milo's age when my mother left my father and took me with her?' he began.

Sam nodded carefully.

Rafaele's mouth became a thin line. 'Unfortunately that day I was subjected to a vision of my father prostrating himself at my mother's feet...begging her not to go. Crying, snivelling. I saw a broken man that day...and I believed for a long time—erroneously—that it had been my mother's fault, that she had done it to him. When, of course, it was much more complicated than that... It didn't help that he blamed her for most of his life, refusing to acknowledge his own part in his downfall.'

Sam took a breath. 'Your father told me a bit...'

Even now her heart ached, because she thought of Milo's pain and distress if he were to witness something like that. How would a scene like that affect a vulnerable, impressionable three-year-old?

But Rafaele didn't seem to hear her. He was looking at the liquid in the glass, swirling it gently. 'And then my stepfather... He was another piece of work. I'd gone from the example of a broken man who had lost everything to living with a man who *had* everything. What they had in common was my mother. They were both obsessed with her, wanted her above all. And she...?' Rafaele smiled grimly. 'She was aloof with them both, but she chose my stepfather over my father because he could provide her with the status and security she'd come to enjoy...'

Rafaele looked at her and his smile became bleak.

'For a long time I never wanted to think about why she did those things...but since I've discovered my older brother and learned she abandoned him I have to realise that perhaps for her, security had become the thing she needed most—above warmth and emotion. Above anything. God knows what happened with her first husband to make her do such a drastic thing as to leave her son, leave his father...'

His mouth twisted.

'From an early age I believed instinctively that women could ruin you *even* if you had money and success. I believed that to succeed *I* had to hold women at the same distance my mother had always done with the men around her. I wouldn't ever be weak like my father or stepfather, and never lose control.'

Rafaele smiled again but it was impossibly bleak.

'And then you came along and slid so deeply under my skin that I didn't realise I'd lost all that precious control until it was too late.'

Sam's heart was beating like a drum now. She felt light-headed. 'I don't... What are you saying, Rafaele?'

He looked at her and his gaze seemed to bore into her. 'I still want us to get married, Sam...'

Something cold settled into her belly. He wasn't going

to let this go. He'd basically just told her how he viewed the women in his life and that only the fact that she'd proved herself to be completely different had merited her this place in his life. She backed away to the door and saw him put down his glass and frown...

'Sam?'

Sam walked out through the door and went to the front door and opened it. Rafaele appeared in the hallway, still frowning.

She shook her head. 'Rafaele, I'm really sorry that you had to see so much at a young age, and that it skewed your views of women... And I can see how Milo is at an age where he must have pushed your buttons... But I can't marry you.'

She forced herself to keep looking at him even though she felt as if a knife was lacerating her insides. 'I want more, Rafaele... Despite what I told you about my views on marriage I've always secretly hoped I'd meet someone and fall in love. I thought I could protect myself too, but I can't...none of us can.'

Rafaele saw Sam backlit in her porch and even in such a domestic banal setting she'd never looked more beautiful. His heart splintered apart into pieces and he knew that he had no choice now but to step out and into the chasm of nothing—*and possibly everything*.

He walked into the middle of the hall and looked at Sam. And then very deliberately he got down on his knees in front of her. For a terrifying moment Rafaele felt the surge of the past threatening to rise up and strangle him, heard voices about to hound him, tell him he was no better than his father... But it didn't happen. What he did feel was a heady feeling of *peace* for the first time in a long time.

Sam was looking at him, horrified. She quickly shut the

door again and leant against it. 'Rafaele, get up… What are you doing?'

Somehow Rafaele found the ability to speak. 'This has been my nightmare scenario for so long, Sam, and I'm tired of it. The truth is that I want more too. I want it all. And I am willing to beg for it—just like my father. Except I know that this is different. I'm not him.'

Sam shook her head and Rafaele could see her eyes grow suspiciously bright.

Her voice sounded thick. 'You don't have to do this just to prove a point. Get *up*, Rafaele…'

He shook his head. The view from down here wasn't bad at all, Rafaele realised. Prostrating himself in front of the woman he loved was something he'd do over and over again if he had to.

Almost gently now, he said, 'Sam…don't you realise it yet?'

She shook her head faintly. 'Realise what?'

Rafaele took a deep breath. 'That I am so madly and deeply and crazily in love with you that I've made a complete mess of everything…'

He looked down for a moment and then back up, steeling himself.

'I know you don't feel the same way…how could you when I've treated you so badly in the past? But… I truly hope that we might have enough to work with…and in time you might feel something. We have Milo…'

Sam just looked at him for a long moment, and then she whispered, 'Did you just say you love me?'

Rafaele nodded, sensing her shock, feeling icicles of pain start to settle around his heart despite his brave words. Humiliation started to make his skin prickle. The demons weren't so far away after all.

Sam closed her eyes and he heard her long, shuddering breath. When she opened them again they overflowed with tears.

'Sam…' he said hoarsely, and went to stand up.

But before he could move she'd launched herself at him and they landed in a tangle of limbs on the floor. The breath was knocked out of Rafaele's chest for a second, and then he saw Sam's face above his own, felt her tears splash onto his cheeks. And he couldn't resist pulling her head down so that he could kiss her. Even in the midst of not knowing, he had to touch her.

The kiss was desperate and salty and wet, and then Sam drew back, breathing hard. She put her hands around his face and said again, 'You love me?'

She was lying on his body, they touched at every point, and Rafaele could feel himself stirring to life. He nodded. 'Yes. I love you, Sam. I want you in my life for ever…you and Milo. I want us to be a family. I can't live without you. When you left last week…I died inside.'

A sob escaped Sam's mouth and Rafaele felt her chest heaving against his.

Finally she managed to get out, 'I love you, Rafaele. I fell for you four years ago, and when you let me go I thought I'd die…but then there was Milo…and I thought I'd stopped loving you and started hating you. But I hadn't. I've always loved you and I will always love you.'

Rafaele sat up and Sam spread her legs around his hips so they faced each other. She sat in the cradle of his lap, where his erection was distractingly full, but he forced himself to look at her, sinking willingly into those grey depths and wondering how on earth he'd not let himself do this before now. It was the easiest thing.

His chest expanded as her words sank in and he felt a very fledgling burgeoning sense of trust take root within him and hold…

'I fell for you too…but it was so terrifying that I ran.

You got too close, Sam—closer than I'd ever let anyone get—and when I realised it I couldn't handle it. Like a coward I left you alone to deal with your trauma...'

Sam smoothed his jaw with a tender hand. She looked at him, her eyes wounded. 'I punished you...in the most heinous way. You were right. I was hurt and upset, heartbroken that you didn't want me... I kept Milo from you, and you didn't deserve that.'

Rafaele tucked some hair behind Sam's ear. He was very serious. 'I understand why you did it. You sensed my reluctance, Sam, my need to escape. But it wasn't from you, it was from myself... You never really left me. You haunted me.'

Sam's eyes flashed. 'Not enough to stop you going to bed with another woman almost immediately.'

Rafaele struggled to comprehend, and then he recalled her accusing him of being with another woman a week after he'd left. He shook his head and smiled wryly, knowing that she was going to demand every inch of him for the rest of his life and not wanting it any other way.

'Would it help you to know that, despite appearances to the contrary I didn't sleep with anyone for a year after you left?' He grimaced. 'I couldn't...perform.'

Sam's eyes widened with obvious feminine satisfaction. 'You were impotent?'

Rafaele scowled. 'I'm not impotent.'

Sam wriggled on his lap, feeling for herself just how potent he was. 'You're not impotent with me.'

Rafaele groaned softly, his hands touching her face, thumb pressing her lower lip. 'I could never be impotent with you. I just have to look at you and I'm turned on.'

Sounding serious, Sam said, 'Me too...'

'Sam...that night when I tied you up...'

A dark flush highlighted those cheekbones and something inside Sam melted anew at seeing him so unlike his

usual confident, cocky self. He was avoiding her eye and
she tipped his chin towards her.

'I liked it…' she whispered, blushing.

'But you cried afterwards…'

Her eyes softened. 'Because I had just realised how
much I still loved you. I felt so vulnerable, and I thought
you were still punishing me for Milo.'

Rafaele groaned. 'I *was* angry, but it was because you
were under my skin again and I didn't want you there. You
brought up too many feelings, made me feel out of control…so I needed to control *you*.'

A wicked glint came into Sam's eyes. 'We can call it
quits if you let me tie you up next time.'

Sam felt Rafaele's body jerk underneath hers.

He quirked a brow at her. 'Bridie has Milo…'

Needing no further encouragement, Sam scrambled in-
elegantly off Rafaele's lap and stood up. She looked down
at him and held out a hand. Rafaele felt his heart squeeze
so much that it hurt. The symbolism of the moment was
huge as he put his hand in Sam's to let her help him up, but
just before he came up all the way, he stopped on one knee.

'Wait…there's one more thing.'

Rafaele's heart beat fast at the way Sam bit her lip. He
gripped her hand like a lifeline and with his other hand
pulled out the small but precious cargo from his pocket.

He held up the vintage diamond ring and looked at her.
'Samantha, will you marry me? Because I love you more
than life itself—you and Milo.'

She looked at the ring and her eyes glittered again with
the onset of fresh tears. 'It's beautiful…'

He could see the final struggle in her face, the fear of
believing that this was *real*…but then she smiled and it
bathed him in a warmth he'd never known before.

'Yes, I'll marry you, Rafaele.'

She held out her hand and it trembled.

With a none too steady hand himself, Rafaele pushed the sparkling ring onto her finger. And then, with his other hand still in her firm grip, she pulled him up out of the painful past and into a brighter future.

A month later...

Sam took a deep breath and started her walk down the aisle of the small church in the grounds of Rafaele's Milan *palazzo*. Umberto was giving her away and he wasn't even using his cane. He was walking taller and stronger almost every day...especially on the days when Bridie was around...

Milo walked ahead of them in a suit, throwing rose petals with chaotic random abandon. He'd look back every now and then with a huge smile and Sam would have to prompt him to keep going. The small church was filled with people, but Sam was oblivious. She saw only the tall figure of the man waiting for her at the top of the aisle. And then he turned around, as if unable to help himself, and he smiled. Sam smiled back.

Umberto handed her over with due deference and then Rafaele was claiming her, pulling her into him. The priest's words washed over and through Sam. She would never have said she was a religious person, but something in the ritual seemed to complete the process she and Rafaele had embarked on a month before, cleansing away any vague residual painful pieces of the past.

There was only now and the future, and the heavy weight of the wedding band on her finger, and Rafaele bending to kiss her with such a look of reverence on his face that she could have wept. In fact she did weep, and he wiped her tears away with his fingers.

Later, as they danced at their reception, which had been

set up in a marquee in the grounds of the *palazzo*, Rafaele said, 'Have I told you yet how beautiful you look?'

Sam smiled. 'About a hundred times, but I don't mind.'

And Sam *felt* beautiful, truly, for the first time in her life. Even though her dress was simple and her hair hadn't been styled by a professional and she'd done her own make-up. She felt confident, and sexy, and most importantly *loved*.

Milo appeared at their feet and Rafaele lifted him up and that was how they finished their wedding dance—in a circle of love, the three of them.

Over in a corner of the marquee stood Alexio Christakos, Rafaele's half-brother. He'd been best man, done his duty and given his speech, made everyone laugh. Made the women giggle and look at him covetously. Even now they surrounded him, waiting for their moment to strike, for the slightest gesture of encouragement.

Alexio grimaced. He was starting to feel claustrophobic. *Hell.* Who was he kidding? He'd been feeling claustrophobic on his brother's behalf ever since Rafaele had told him that he was getting married and had a *son!*

He shook his head again and grimaced when he saw Rafaele kiss his bride for the umpteenth time. Alexio looked at her. He guessed she was pretty enough, in a subtle and unassuming way, but he couldn't see how she made Rafaele turn almost feral whenever another man came close. Even Alexio had been sent none too subtle hands-off signals from the moment he'd met her.

Alexio wondered how it was possible that Rafaele couldn't see that she *must* be marrying him only for his security and wealth. Had he become so duped by good sex that he'd forgotten one of the most important lessons they'd learnt from their dear departed mother? That a woman's main aim in life was to feather her nest and seek the security of a rich man?

Alexio mentally saluted his brother and wished him well. He told himself he'd try not to say *I told you so* when it all fell apart. Mind you, he had to concede the kid was cute. *His nephew.* He'd actually had quite an entertaining time with him earlier, when he'd looked after him for a bit between the wedding and the reception. Still… He shuddered lightly. He had no intention of embarking on that path any time soon, if ever…

Alexio stopped focusing on his brother and his new wife and son for a minute and took in the crowd around him. From nearby, a gorgeous brunette caught his eye. She was tall and lissom, with curves in all the right places. She looked at him with sexy confidence and smiled the smile of a practised seductress.

Alexio felt his body stir, his blood move southwards. It wasn't the most compelling spark of attraction he'd ever felt…*but when was the last time that had happened…?* Alexio ignored that voice and smiled back. When he saw the light of triumph in her eyes at catching the attention of the most eligible bachelor in the room, Alexio forced down the feeling of emptiness inside him and moved towards her.

* * * * *

A sneaky peek at next month…

MODERN™

POWER, PASSION AND IRRESISTIBLE TEMPTATION

My wish list for next month's titles…

In stores from 21st February 2014:

❏ A Prize Beyond Jewels – Carole Mortimer

❏ Pretender to the Throne – Maisey Yates

❏ The Sheikh's Last Seduction – Jennie Lucas

❏ The Woman Sent to Tame Him – Victoria Parker

In stores from 7th March 2014:

❏ A Queen for the Taking? – Kate Hewitt

❏ An Exception to His Rule – Lindsay Armstrong

❏ Enthralled by Moretti – Cathy Williams

❏ What a Sicilian Husband Wants – Michelle Smart

Available at WHSmith, Tesco, Asda, Eason, Amazon and Apple

Just can't wait?

Special Offers

Every month we put together collections and longer reads written by your favourite authors.

Here are some of next month's highlights— and don't miss our fabulous discount online!

On sale 21st February   On sale 28th February   On sale 21st February

 # *Save 20%*
on all Special Releases

The Royal
HOUSE OF KAREDES

Join the Mills & Boon Book Club

Want to read more **Modern**™ books?
We're offering you **2 more** absolutely **FREE!**

We'll also treat you to these fabulous extras:

- Exclusive offers and much more!

- FREE home delivery

- FREE books and gifts with our special rewards scheme

Get your free books now!

visit www.millsandboon.co.uk/bookclub
or call Customer Relations on 020 8288 2888

Discover more romance at

www.millsandboon.co.uk

- ❤ WIN great prizes in our exclusive competitions
- ❤ BUY new titles before they hit the shops
- ❤ BROWSE new books and REVIEW your favourites
- ❤ SAVE on new books with the Mills & Boon® Bookclub™
- ❤ DISCOVER new authors

PLUS, to chat about your favourite reads, get the latest news and find special offers:

- ❤ Find us on facebook.com/millsandboon
- ❤ Follow us on twitter.com/millsandboonuk
- ❤ Sign up to our newsletter at millsandboon.co.uk